During the Fall

Cheryl Murnane

CHERYL MURNANE PUBLISHING

Copyright © Cheryl Murnane, 2014

Date of first printing: May 2014

ISBN: 978-0-9903862-0-9

Print layout by Guido Henkel, www.guidohenkel.com

For all the strong women in my life,
especially Mom and Nan,
who showed me everything is possible

Jenny

I WAS SIXTEEN YEARS OLD WHEN I FELL IN LOVE WITH ALEX MURPHY. Yes, I was young, but even then I recognized the depth of our love. We have been through a lot in our years together, and we have built a lasting connection on love and respect. I wouldn't be me without him in my life. I try to hold onto the faith my grandmother taught me and to believe everything will turn out right. But some problems seem impossible, and faith — well, it seems to slip past me, no matter how hard I try to hold on.

As a teenager, I didn't know what I wanted to do with my life. I stayed away from trouble, but lacked the direction and drive many of my friends shared. From a young age, I knew I wanted to have a strong marriage and a family. I'd had a few boyfriends, but no one was special enough to keep around, so I focused my attention on schoolwork, community service, and my friends.

I spent weekends helping out at the community center, where my church organized community service opportunities for teens. On Saturdays, I went to the center and worked with children who needed help with schoolwork. When that was done, we drew colorful pictures and created arts and crafts like personalized buttons or glass suncatchers. All the while, thoughts of motherhood floated in my mind. The time I spent with the kids in the community center reinforced my desire to have a family of my own.

After leaving the center for the day, I would meet up with my friends. Our town was so small it took less than ten minutes to drive from one end to other. After driving around, looking for a place to park and hang out without being bothered, we always seemed to end up at someone's house to watch a movie and eat all the junk food we could stuff in before getting sick. Being a teenager was great, and I enjoyed the freedoms my parents gave me, but a feeling of emptiness haunted my soul.

The high school I went to included students from two adjacent towns. There were more than thirteen hundred students, and it seemed every day you could meet someone new. I will never forget the first time I met Alex. Alex Murphy was the star athlete in hockey and baseball, so I knew his name — everyone knew his name — but I was involved in my own life, often lost in the many books I read. I wasn't an athlete and didn't follow the school sports teams, so there was no reason for me to realize how good-looking he was or anything more about the super-star athlete. But that all changed one afternoon when I saw him in the school cafeteria with his friends.

Carrying my books, I came around the corner of the cafeteria. Roars of laughter filled the air, mixed with humming chatter, moving like a cloud above the heads of the lunch crowd. The sound of pure joy drew my attention.

I scanned the room for the source of the electrifying amusement and saw a group of students gathered around a table. I felt my stomach flip when I saw him standing above the kids at the table. They all looked up at Alex. His presence commanded their attention. All eyes were on him, and they were clearly mesmerized. He stood with his hands in his pockets, telling them something that caused fits of laughter. He was tall, with brown wavy hair that fell over his ears. His jeans revealed the tightness of his butt. I got lost staring at it and had to blink, hoping no one saw me gawking. His black t-shirt fit him perfectly. I could tell he worked out because his muscles flexed every time he laughed.

I was not shy, and as I stood staring at the group, I decided I had waited long enough. A yearning drew me toward him, I was hyper-aware of my senses and of my surroundings, and suddenly overwhelmed by the desire to be near him. I was intrigued. I took a deep breath and walked over to the group.

"Hi, I'm Jenny." I stood next to the table, slightly in front of him, waiting to hear him speak. He turned and met my gaze. My palms started to sweat and my heart raced. I thought to myself that I was in love.

He seemed struck by my presence, too. As we stood face to face, he stared into my eyes, and the strong energy between us radiated through me powerfully. His cologne wafted over me, the smell of beach sand mixed with a woody masculine fragrance. I felt comfortable standing next to him, but my body was tingling and my hearing became muffled. It was as if the crowd was moving in slow motion and the only people in real time were me and Alex. My heart didn't stop racing, and my palms were still moist. I stared at him, waiting to hear his voice, hoping it would calm me down.

"I'm Alex."

His friends couldn't help but sense the energy moving between us. Time seemed to stand still, and then I felt intoxicated. Trying to break his stare, I looked around and noticed that everyone was staring at us, waiting and watching to see what would happen next.

I began to feel nervous, not so confident now, and needed to end the silence. I said to him, "I could hear laughter from around the corner. I had to see where it was coming from and what it was about."

He fumbled for words, as if he did not know what to say. The next thing I knew, he was introducing me to the friends sitting closest to us. "I'm sorry… This is Mark and Diane." Turning to the boy sitting on the other side of him, he introduced me to Bill, his best friend.

Appreciating the distraction, I looked at his friends and said, "Hi. It's nice to meet you guys." A moment later the bell rang, ending the lunch period, but everyone continued to stare at Alex and me. Then they began to reluctantly get up from the table, almost tripping over themselves, not wanting to turn away from what might happen between the two of us.

Kids pushed past us, but Alex and I stood there smiling at each other, not speaking. I couldn't read him. He looked lost in thought. I was uncertain about what to say or do, so I looked down at my shoes. When I looked up again, into Alex's eyes, I scratched my head and said, "Well, uh, I need to be in English in two minutes. It was nice meeting you, Alex."

"Yeah, you too," he said.

I could tell he was distracted. By what, I didn't know.

I walked down the long, crowded hallway to English, bumping into just about everyone who passed me. It was like I was floating above the ground; every step felt softer than the reality that I was walking on the concrete pad beneath the tiled floor. I had never felt a sensation like that before. I hoped I would always remember the first time I met Alex.

Sitting in English class, my thoughts about the guy I just met in the cafeteria raced all over the place. *Why did he stand there, not speaking*, I wondered. He'd just stared at me. I wondered if he'd felt the same electric sensation rushing through his veins as I had. It would surprise me if he hadn't. I wondered if he thought I was pretty. Everyone always told me how beautiful I was, but I thought I was just average. My brown hair is long and wavy, cut just below my shoulders, a style shared by lots of girls. I'm five feet, five inches tall...average. At my last doctor's appointment I weighed 120 pounds—again, average. But I knew my eyes were anything but average. I have my grandmother's eyes, a mix of light chocolate tones with caramel accents running through them. They were the one thing that set me apart from the other brunette girls I knew.

I've seen people become lost in my eyes. Cashiers smile at me, staring, and then comment on how stunning my eyes are. My friends' parents have remarked on the amazing color of my eyes. Many times people start to talk to me, only to look up, notice my eyes, and lose their train of thought. I wondered if it might have been the same with

Alex. If so, the energy moving between us had to have made an impact on him.

I noticed my heart started to race when I thought about being near him, a new feeling for me. I have never been in love, but I was sure I was falling in love with Alex.

"Jenny, are you with us? Do you know what the answer is?" my English teacher called, tearing me away from my thoughts about Alex. I was speechless and blushed as I started fumbling for the answer. But I hadn't heard the question. My teacher shook her head and moved on. Embarrassed, I covered my face with my hands.

Alex

I WAS LEFT STANDING ALONE, MY FEET FROZEN TO THE FLOOR. First I was speechless, and now I'm not sure which way to go. What just happened to me? One minute I'm hanging out with my friends and the next there is this naturally beautiful girl standing in front of me, making me lose my shit. I couldn't explain why I felt that strong pull toward her. I couldn't find words; my mind was blank, and my mouth was dry. She caught me by surprise. No one has ever done that to me before. I'm always ready for people and new situations; I'm usually quick to react, and I always have something to say.

But something about her caused my mind to go blank. Her eyes locked in on mine and everything else went away like it was just the two of us standing there. My heart raced and I started to sweat. Like an idiot, the only thing I could manage to do was introduce her to my friends. Great first impression I made. And then the bell rang before I could pull myself together, and she walked away. As she did, I felt some part of me go with her.

"Hey, Alex. Hello…Alex?"

I blinked and noticed my baseball coach in front of me. I was standing in the field, but I couldn't remember getting there. The sun was shining in my eyes and I felt the warmth from the springtime sun on my skin. My teammates and I began running through our drills, but I couldn't get the image of her eyes out of my mind. Every time I blinked, she flashed before me. She was smiling and looking into my eyes. I felt a surge of energy race through my veins, and I had a hard time focusing on practice.

Jenny was wrapped up in my thoughts. The harder I tried to not think about her, the more intense my thoughts became. I had to see her again. That's when I realized something — how would I find her again? I didn't know her last name, only her first name — Jenny. There were a lot of Jennys at school. I thought about her name, and pictured her standing in front of me, so confident. She was a beautiful girl with an average name. I couldn't think of anything else that was average about her. I would just have to wait until tomorrow and hope to see her again in the cafeteria.

That night, I lay in bed thinking about her, I couldn't sleep. When I did manage to fall asleep, she appeared in every dream. As I tossed and turned, I couldn't get her out of my mind. The way she smiled at me with that sparkle in her eye drove me nuts. I'd had girlfriends; most were casual relationships lasting a few months. I put all my focus on schoolwork and practicing and playing sports. My parents had dreams for me to continue in my grandfather's path by becoming a professional hockey player. Coaches told me I had talent and should push myself to be better. Like every little boy who dreams of becoming a superstar athlete, I was determined to break through all the barriers that would try to hold me back and stop me from achieving my goals. I thought that there was no way I was going to let anything or anyone stop me, but the problem was the impact Jenny made on me. After meeting her, I knew my life was about to change.

Jenny

ALEX AND I STARTED DATING A FEW DAYS AFTER WE MET IN THE cafeteria, and our connection grew deeper every day and during the year that followed. We spent every possible minute together, but spare time was hard to find because Alex was constantly playing sports. I learned about his goals and dreams, and I didn't want to get in the way. He was focused on his plan to become a professional athlete; I didn't know exactly where I would fit in with his plan. I knew he loved me. I could feel it when we were together, but I questioned if our relationship would last if he went away to college.

Deep down, I didn't want Alex to turn pro, although I kept my opinions inside. I couldn't live with myself if I was the one to prevent his dreams from coming true, but I couldn't deny that I was anxious when I thought about the lifestyle I would live as his girlfriend, and maybe someday as his wife, if he was intensely focused on hockey and traveling with his team.

I talked to my Aunt Sally, my mother's younger sister and my surrogate big sister. She told me, Jenny, you need to realize that you can never know for sure what your or Alex's future holds. But for the time being, honey, you're lucky to have Alex in your life. He's a love of a lifetime. A person doesn't always find one.

She hugged me and always knew how to comfort me. I didn't know what I would do without her in my life.

I cherished the moments I spent with Alex. With graduation only months away, our lives would be changing all too soon. As we walked hand and hand around the mall, Alex asked me to the senior prom. Of course, I said yes.

The day of the prom arrived. I was so nervous, I couldn't stop shaking. Aunt Sally arranged to bring me to her hairstylist for a makeover, so I would look perfect for Alex.

"Jenny, how do you feel about adding some highlights to frame your face and compliment the caramel tones in your hair?" Richard asked. He wrung his hands together like a praying mantis, waiting to attack my head and recreate whatever vision he had seen in a trendy magazine.

I had no idea what he was talking about. I thanked God I had my aunt there. I trusted her; she seemed to know just what he meant.

"Richard, that sounds perfect. I knew I could trust you to take care of her." My aunt stroked my hair. I sat confined in his styling chair while they discussed my makeover.

After three hours and a lot attention, Richard spun the chair around to reveal my new look and I could hardly recognize the girl staring back at me. My eyelids were colored with blue eye shadow, and my hair had volume I never thought possible. I knew Richard had done his job. I looked almost perfect; all that was left was to put on my dress. I had no doubts that Alex would think I was the prettiest girl at the prom.

My aunt couldn't contain her tears. "Oh, Jenny. Look at you, honey—you look beautiful. Do you like it?" I knew I held a special place in my aunt's heart. She never wanted to see me upset. I knew she loved me. Probably more than most aunts love their nieces.

"Yes, Aunt Sally. Thank you, I love it!" My smile was so big I was afraid my makeup would crack.

The clock in our kitchen struck five just as the doorbell rang, Alex was right on schedule. I waited in the family room near the fireplace to take pictures. As Alex and my father approached, butterflies swarmed in my stomach. Alex was talking with my father, but became distracted when he saw me.

"Wow! Jenny, you look amazing." I could tell Alex enjoyed the new me.

"So do you in your tuxedo—big change from your jeans and t-shirts!"

Alex placed the pink and purple corsage around my wrist.

We arrived at the prom in a limo, ready to dance and eat—although we did more dancing than eating. Alex's best friend, Bill, and his date won the contest for most original moves. It came as no surprise that Alex and I were crowned prom king and queen. After all, he was the captain of the hockey team, and our school held the hockey team in high regard. As his girlfriend, I was a shoe-in for the Queen.

As prom king and queen, Alex and I danced to Peter Gabriel's song "In Your Eyes." If my world had stopped at that moment, I would have died the happiest person in the room. Alex was everything I had ever dreamed my boyfriend would be; he was considerate and funny. As he held me close and we moved in unison, I felt happy to have him in life.

"Jenny, I never want this night to end. You look so beautiful. I am the luckiest boy here tonight." He held me in his arms, and I prayed he'd never let me go.

"Alex, tonight has been perfect."

With graduation only a month away, I had been thinking a lot about the fall. Alex would leave for college, and we would have to say our good-byes. I didn't want to ruin a perfect night, but before I could stop myself the words left my mouth. "I wish we could stay like this forever and you wouldn't have to leave me to go to college."

He sensed the hurt in my voice, and he was concerned. "Jenny, have you been worried about me leaving?" He stood straight and looked down into my eyes.

"Alex, now isn't the time to talk about it. Sorry I let it slip out. Let's talk about it another time."

"Okay, another time." His expression was apprehensive, but he nodded and we silently floated around the dance floor in harmony.

By the spring of our senior year, everyone I was close to had accepted offers to go to college. Some would be close to home; others decided to go far away. During my senior year, something had changed in me. As the time grew near to apply to schools, fears about leaving the comfort of my family crept in, and I had decided I wasn't going to live away at college just because everyone else was.

My love of children led me to my interest in taking classes for early childhood development. My parents supported my decision. My mother loved the notion that I would stay at home and commute to school. I enrolled in a nearby college to become certified to teach; it was the quickest way to start my career helping to shape and make a difference in the lives of young children.

When the day came for my first class, I was filled with excitement. I had bought all my new school supplies: pencils, notebooks, folders, and the like. Dressed in my new college clothes, I felt like an adult. Heading out the door that crisp fall morning, I yelled good-bye to my mother. With eager anticipation I started my car, wondering how college would be.

As I drove the twenty minutes to my new school, I was aware of every nerve ending in my body. I turned on the radio and started flipping channels in hopes of finding music to calm the mixture of nerves and anticipation I felt over not knowing anyone in my classes. I was excited to meet new people knowing all my friends were away now; I hoped that meeting new people would bring fresh richness to my life. Walking up to the building gave me time to pull myself together and shake off the first-day-of-school jitters. I approached the brick building with confidence, knowing I was heading to the correct building. It had been a smart idea to give up a day at the beach to tour the campus that summer.

Surrounded by other students, as I got closer to the building I said a prayer and walked into my first college class.

That night at dinner my parents asked about my day. With excitement I shared my experiences of the day, bit by bit, sparing no detail.

"I'm off to a great start. My teachers seem great. They're very en-thusiastic about teaching. I know I made the right choice to work with little kids."

"Jenny, we're happy to hear that." Between bites my dad asked, "Have you heard from Alex?"

"No, I haven't." I said. I twirled the spaghetti around and around on my fork, trying to coat it with as much Parmesan cheese as possible. "I bet he's just busy trying to get settled in and all. He'll call soon, I hope." Then dread washed over me as I thought about what Alex could be doing to keep him from calling me.

While I helped to clean up after dinner, I started to worry again about my relationship with Alex. How could we continue to have a real relationship when Alex was so far away? I hated to think about the pretty girls that might flirt with him. He was so modest—he didn't realize how gorgeous he was. I knew most girls would do anything to be with him. I became nauseated from the ideas floating around in my head. I needed to hear his voice; it had been days since we spoke.

I stared out into the back yard as I scrubbed the dishes. I recalled the night I spent with Alex before he left for school. The mid-August air was warm. As we walked barefoot on the patio, I felt the heat it had absorbed from the hot summer sun during the day; every step I took relaxed my feet. We laid on chaise lounges and looked up at the stars that twinkled in the black sky. I tried hard to push away the thought that this was the last night that Alex and I would sit under the same night sky. Instead I forced myself to appreciate the last moments we had together. I scrubbed the dish harder, and then my dog walked into the kitchen and interrupted my memories. God, I missed him.

I left the dishes and picked up the phone to call him.

"Hello?" A boy answered the phone. Alex's roommate, I guessed.

"Hi, this is Jenny. Is Alex Murphy there?" I fought to keep my voice smooth.

"Hold on. He's not in the room, but I'll look for him."

While I waited for the boy to find Alex, I twisted the phone cord around my finger, and then I remembered that my father hated it when my brother and I did that.

I heard footsteps and the sound of the phone moving in someone's hand. "I can't find him, but I'll tell him you called. You said your name is Jenny, right?"

"Yes. Jenny. Please don't forget to tell him. Thanks." The pit in my stomach was growing larger; what could he be doing instead of answering my call?

I sat at the kitchen table and thought about how differently things had turned out from how we'd planned a year ago. During the fall of our senior year, Alex talked about taking classes at the local college to study engineering. That way we could go to college and still be together and continue to work to achieve our dreams. But when a Michigan State recruiter called his hockey coach, everything changed.

As Alex's last high school hockey season unfolded, the team earned first place in their division. Alex, the captain and leading scorer, drew the attention of many college hockey recruiters with his impressive numbers. It had always been his dream to play professional hockey and to follow in his grandfather's footsteps. He had played with the Hartford Whalers before his career ended early due to an injury. Alex loved his grandfather and wanted to make him proud, so he'd made it his goal to work as hard as he could to match the status his grandfather had achieved.

The call he made to me as the hockey season was ending had been hard to take.

"Hey, Jenny. I need to talk to you about something," he had said.

From the tone of his voice I could tell it wasn't good news. "What's up?" I said, trying to sound cheerful.

"Well, you know there's been a lot of talk about my hockey skills. Recruiters are showing up to my games." He paused, "God, this is hard to tell you."

I could tell he was trying to soften the blow that was coming my way. "Just say it, Alex. What is it?"

"My parents and I met with the recruiter and the head coach from Michigan State today."

"And?"

"Jenny, they offered me a full scholarship to play hockey for them, and um, well, I accepted it."

There it was—it was out. The words hung in the air. It was awful—he was leaving. I tried to hold back my tears, but as I started to speak, the only sounds that came out of me were sobs and gasps for air. I thought about all our time together and the dreams we shared; now they would be gone. Without Alex here with me next year I would have to find new dreams and a new life, but I didn't want that. I wanted Alex and our dreams. I knew I was being selfish. This was his dream, a dream he'd had long before we fell in love.

I took a deep breath and tried to calm myself down. I said, "That's great!" I was trying to cover up the sadness in my voice and hoped he couldn't hear it. "So you're going to Michigan. You must be very happy."

"Jenny, are you okay? I'm sorry to do this to you. I know we had plans to go to school around here and be together, but this…" There was silence. "This is the beginning of my dreams coming true. We'll make it work. Okay?"

At that point it was just easier to agree. "Okay."

I had lain in bed that night, thinking. Alex had earned himself a hockey scholarship to Michigan State. He would be thirteen hours away by car and a few hours by airplane, but between studying, practicing, and games, he would have no time to come home to see me. Even if I were to visit him, he wouldn't have spare time to spend with me. I started to doubt our magical romance was going to last long. How could it survive the distance without time together? We could talk on the telephone and send "I love you" letters, but we wouldn't be able to touch each other, to feel each other's skin and look into each other's eyes.

Weeks after I found out Alex was going to Michigan State, I decided I should apply to their education department. When I was accepted, I didn't tell Alex. I thought about sharing the news with him but chose not to because I wasn't ready to leave home. I knew he would want me to go, but I wasn't about to chase him to Michigan like some insecure little girl. I was certain I wasn't ready to be far from home, and I knew his time at college would be consumed with classes and hockey. We loved each other, and if our love were meant to be, it would survive four years apart—and the distance. It would prepare us for life when he went pro.

On the night of my first day of college, I tossed and turned in my bed and suddenly wondered if I had made a mistake by not accepting the Michigan State offer. Here I was, at home, and Alex was a thousand miles away—with girls. He was so good-looking, with his wavy hair that called to be touched and the sweet smile that could melt any girl's heart. His easy-going personality put people at ease; you couldn't help but feel relaxed in his presence. I knew they would all want him, I cringed at the thought of them throwing themselves at him. *What is keeping him from calling me back?* I tried to convince myself that the roommate forgot to tell him and prayed that's all that it was.

January to May was the hardest part of our first year apart. After I completed my classes and homework, the days grew long and boring. Alex was deep into his hockey schedule, unable to come home, and we rarely spoke more than ten minutes a day. He often insisted it wasn't worth going out to visit him because he had no free time. But in the beginning of March, he called with the great news. "Hi, Jenny. Do you have plans next weekend? My coach gave us the weekend off from practice, so I'm free until Monday. I would love for you to come here so I can spend time with you."

I jumped when I heard his invitation. "I can take the last flight Thursday night. I don't have classes on Friday. Alex, I can't wait to see you."

"I know—it's been way too long. The school year will be over in about two months, and then we can be together all summer."

I wanted to go see him so badly. It felt like forever since he had been home at Christmas time. I had started to consider transferring there after all because I felt if I wanted to keep our love alive I had to be closer to him.

I was finally ready to explore new places and put some distance between me and my hometown. It turned out that most of my classmates weren't interested in hanging out after school because they had jobs, so I didn't make many new friends. My social life was nonexistent. My parents supported my tentative plans to transfer; they saw I was unhappy and thought I should have the full college experience. They recommended that I tour the campus and the area. Then I would have all the information I needed to make a final decision.

The weekend Alex and I spent together was amazing. I fell in love with the college campus. I visited the hockey arena and met Alex's hockey coach. Alex's friends were very welcoming. I spoke with students who were taking classes in the education department and they gave positive reviews of their courses. After I met Alex's friends and walked around the campus, my mind was made up. I would finish the year in Massachusetts and start the fall semester in Michigan. After I finalized the details with my parents and both colleges, I would tell Alex.

Alex

WHEN JENNY CAME INTO MY LIFE, EVERYTHING CHANGED. I struggled with how to reconcile my love for hockey and my love for Jenny, but I knew the scholarship to Michigan State would allow the right people to follow my career and showcase my talents to the professional hockey draft board. All my dreams were falling into place, and I couldn't have been more thrilled.

I thought our love was strong enough to handle anything, but after my first semester I realized I wouldn't be able to both have a relationship with Jenny and focus on my hockey season. I questioned if I could juggle both. By the end of my freshmen year, I knew I had to let Jenny go. We tried all the strategies that long-distance couples do: we wrote letters and talked on the phone and satisfied our desires on the phone too. It got the job done, but there was no substitute for touching my girlfriend's body and feeling her warm skin under my hands and smelling her sweetness as we look into each other's eyes.

I had agonized over my decision for weeks. I wondered if my love for Jenny had changed over the year we spent away from each other. Not being able to spend time together made me question if were we still in love with each other or just with the idea of who we once were. I enjoyed having her visit, but I couldn't lead her on with a dream that was becoming harder and harder to sustain. She deserved more; she deserved a man who would be there to hold her and laugh with her. Someone she could see, show her love for, and give her love to.

The semester was almost over, and students were beginning to pack up their rooms. Knowing I would be going home in a couple weeks was bittersweet. I couldn't wait to see my family. It had been months since I was home, and I really missed my bed. And then there was Jenny. I appreciated the richness she brought to my life. She showed me there was more to life than hockey, and she opened my eyes to a love so rich, I knew I could never love like that again. I was forever changed. I became a better person because of her, and I knew she deserved better than what I was giving her.

The plane ride home was sickening, and I had knots in my stomach. I stared out the window as we flew over the towns and roadways below, laid out in simple squares and rectangular patterns, feeling as small as an ant. I was on the fence about how to end it with Jenny. I contemplated whether I should end it right away and start moving on and try to get over her or wait till the end of summer and enjoy myself until then. Either way she was going to get hurt; I was going to leave her with a broken heart. But maybe she sensed it was coming. I couldn't know for sure; during our conversations we talked about our love and how much we missed each other and how difficult it was to be apart. We still had love for each other, even though we had only seen each other twice during the college year.

I reclined my seat and closed my eyes, envisioning Jenny standing at the gate waiting for me. She would look amazing, her brown hair down around her shoulders. As I moved closer to her I would smell her sweet scent; she always smelled like gardenias. It was a warm May afternoon, so she would probably be wearing a sundress, revealing her curves. I hadn't held her in my arms in months, but I didn't forget how she fit. With her head resting on my chest, she would be able to hear my heart racing. Her arms would wrap around my waist and pull me into her body. I loved the feeling of holding her close. Man, I missed feeling her next to me. I had to shake the image out of my mind. I was driving myself nuts.

I adjusted myself and I sat up in my seat as the plane began its descent. I decided to wait and see how my plan would unfold, and try to pick the right time to talk to Jenny about our relationship. With a deep breath, I walked out of the gate into the airport. I raced with the other passengers to the baggage claim area. Speed didn't work to my benefit because my luggage was the last piece off. I stood breathlessly waiting for my bag to appear as the other passengers lifted their luggage and found their families, friends, or taxi drivers. The clicking and shuffling of the conveyer belt kept me entertained while I watched for my bags.

When I finally lifted my bags from the conveyer belt, the crowd began to thin out. I turned to locate the best exit to find Jenny. As people gathered their belongings and moved about, an opening was created and there she was. My knees buckled when I saw Jenny. She was wearing a blue sundress and looked better than I had imagined.

"Alex!" she yelled, waving her arms. Her voice sounded like an angel's.

As I walked toward her, I smiled. The surprised look on her face told me she noticed I had cut my hair. She ran up to me, and I dropped my bags and picked her up. The force of her jump into my arms sent us spinning in a circle. We laughed. It felt good to be with her again. I separated from her and held her face in my hands, looking her in the eyes and wetting my lips just a bit with my tongue. I leaned in to place the most sensual kiss on her mouth; my body became alive as my lips moved over hers and I felt all of my love pour out of me and into her. I could have taken her to the ground right there in the middle of the airport to show her how much I missed her.

Breaking away, I looked into her mesmerizing eyes, and a knot tightened in my stomach. How could I diminish the twinkle that shone so brightly in her eyes? It hurt me to know I would break her heart. Before I could speak, she filled the silence.

"Alex, you've grown up! You look like a man. Your hair is gone! I love the new style," she said as she ran her hands through my shorter hair, waking every nerve ending on my scalp.

"Thanks. Sorry that I didn't tell you." Feeling guilty, I ran my hand through the hair left on my head.

"But something else is different too." She looked at me with a concerned look on her face. "Are you okay?"

"Yeah. Everything's fine." I wasn't ready to talk about the end of our relationship. Not at this point, with the girl I loved and hadn't seen in months standing in front of me making me harder than stone. No way. It would have to wait. I was going to put off what I had to do.

As we walked hand in hand out of the airport, I told her, "I've missed you so much, Jenny. It's seems like a dream to be touching you, looking at you, and smelling you. You are still wearing the same gardenia perfume, aren't you?"

"Yes. I know how much you love it." She squeezed my hand. "I can't believe it either—you're actually here with me! It's been so lonely without you. I can't wait to spend every minute with you. I hope your parents don't mind," she said. She bumped me with her shoulder.

"I guess we'll have to see what they say." I bumped her back.

"What are we going to do first, Alex?"

"Are your parents' home? Maybe we could start there." I raised my eyebrows and smiled at her. She knew what the look in my eyes meant. I could tell by the look on her face she was thinking the same thing.

"Alex, its morning. I have your breakfast ready!" my mother called from the bottom of the stairs. What a welcome—my first morning back, and she'd cooked breakfast for me. I stumbled from my bed, sporting really bad bed hair. My shorter hair stuck up in all directions when I woke up in the morning. I pulled on a t-shirt and shorts and headed to the kitchen.

"Good morning, honey. It's great to have you home. I missed making these big breakfasts. You know your sister. She wouldn't dare eat bacon, sausage, and home fries."

I sat down at the table, preoccupied. I asked, "Can I talk to you about something, Mom?" I was unsure how to start the conversation, but I knew my mother would help me make sense of the concerns I had about Jenny. "I think I need to end things with Jenny."

My mother turned quickly from cleaning the frying pan, her mouth open, and gasped. "Are things okay? I thought you two were doing great."

Well, it's just that…um. Mom, I don't know." I dropped my fork onto my plate, frustration building inside of me.

"Slow down, Alex. Tell me what you mean." She sat across from me at the table.

"Mom, I still love her. I realized that yesterday when I saw her at the airport. She makes me feel whole when we're together. It's just that school and hockey are taking over my life, and I don't see how she fits into my life now." I knew my mom could see the hurt and confusion in my eyes.

My mother took a deep breath and said, "Alex, Jenny may not fit into your school life, but she is a huge part of your life. Give it some more time. If it is meant to be, you will survive the distance and your schedule. The first year of anything new is the hardest. Nothing can destroy true love, Alex."

I looked up at her and thought, *She's right*. I could enjoy the summer with Jenny—at least.

Jenny

ALEX ARRIVED AT MY HOUSE AT ABOUT ELEVEN, JUST AS THE SUN began its climb to the highest point of the sky. It was a perfect summer day. The sun was illuminating the world around me, and a slight breeze blew the warm air through the leaves on the trees; the birds were calling to each other.

Alex and I were going to meet some friends at the beach. I came out of the house wearing my new beach cover-up, a white crochet dress that revealed my skin and my bright pink bikini — it didn't actually cover very much. I think Alex liked it; I heard him whistle out the car window as I walked down the walkway. I curtsied and slid into the passenger seat.

"Nice dress. When did you get that? I like it," he said. Then he slid his hand up my thigh as I buckled my seatbelt.

He seemed more into what was underneath the dress than the dress itself. "Hey, watch it!" I said, slapping his hand away. "We have to pick up Ben and meet the others at the beach."

"Okay, okay. I'll get you later." He looked at me with a smile. "Are your parents cool with you being gone all day?"

"Oh, yeah. They're working until six and then meeting each other for dinner. So I'm all yours." I took his hand from my leg placed it on the steering wheel.

He leaned over and kissed me. I kissed him back and gave him a tight hug. "I'm so glad you're home."

We tiptoed over the scorching hot sand to where some friends were setting up tents and chairs. Ben set up the hibachi grill up near one of the tents; Alex placed our bags and cooler next to it. More kids began to show up, and they started sharing stories about the year they'd spent at college. Of course, all the guys were asking Alex about his school, but they mostly wanted to know about hockey.

The girls were talking about the cute older guys they met, and some were telling stories about drinking at the bars and going back to their dorms with guys they had met. After spending the night together, they never saw them again. I was disgusted by the thought. I sat there, unsure how to feel. I could not relate to anything our friends were talking about. I could have gone away to college, but I chose to stay home and commute because I didn't need to be part of that scene. I had a boyfriend, one who loved me and would never disgrace me like the boys they were talking about. I didn't fit into their conversation.

"I'm going for a walk." I couldn't sit and listen to any more.

"Wait, Jenny. I'll come with you," Alex said.

As we walked along the shoreline for the first time that season, we felt the icy water wash over our toes. I heard Alex's voice over the wind. "Hey, what's going on, Jenny?"

I gathered my hair away from face and tied it in a loose knot on my head. "I don't fit in with our friends anymore. Everyone has crazy stories about school, and I have nothing to add. No exciting party stories or drunken debaucheries. Why would anyone want to hear about my commute or the time I spend hanging out at the Java Bean? That's so last year. And I haven't even stepped foot into a bar!" Feeling sorry for myself, I continued rambling. "It's just that I feel like I don't relate to the group anymore. Everyone's talking about school. I'm the only one at home, commuting."

"That's what you wanted, Jenny."

I stopped and turned to face Alex. "Well, maybe it's what I thought I wanted, Alex."

"What are you saying?"

"I'm ready to go away to college."

"Really? Where would you go?"

Looking him in the eye I told him, "Michigan State."

"With me?" He didn't see that coming.

"Yes, with you. I couldn't stand being away from you this year—it was horrible. I am only half myself when you're not here. I never told you I applied there last year and was accepted, but I turned them down. I realized too late that I made a mistake. When you left after the holidays, I knew it would be summer before I saw you again, and it made me sick. Then you invited me out, so I got to see the school, and I loved it. I reapplied and got in."

Picking me up in his arms, Alex held me close. The sun beat down on us, and waves crashed around his legs. "Jenny, I would love to have you at Michigan State. I can't wait for the fall, to have you at school with me. Oh, I'm so happy, Jenny!"

I sensed a sudden feeling of joy come over him. He seemed more relaxed, and over the sound of crashing waves and seagulls squawking, I thought I heard I him whisper, "It will all work out after all."

Alex

THE YEARS JENNY SPENT WITH ME AT COLLEGE FILLED THE HOLE I had experienced without her there. I enjoyed seeing her in the morning for a brief time before we went to our classes; a day that started with seeing Jenny made me feel content all day. During my hockey games, I was thrilled that she was in the stands watching and cheering my team and me on. Having Jenny at college kept our love alive.

Jenny joined a reading club through the library and volunteered at the local elementary school to assist with a math leadership program. It was a challenge to find time to spend together, but we managed to use our free time to be with each other. Whenever we could, we would sneak away from our friends to enjoy a quiet night at the movies or just hang out in one of our dorm rooms talking and dreaming about our future. Our dreams included my desire to design our house and Jenny's desire to have a family in it.

In the fall of our junior year, Jenny's Aunt Sally came for a visit, and Jenny was thrilled to see her again. She couldn't wait to show her aunt around the campus and have her meet her new friends. But, secretly, I knew Jenny was looking forward to having her aunt spoil her. Whenever the two of them got together it always involved shopping.

On the day we picked Sally up from the airport there wasn't a cloud in the sky, and her flight was on time. Jenny was shaking like a little child waiting for a gift, and when Sally found us by the exit doors Jenny ran up to hug her.

"Aunt Sally, you're here!"

"Hi Jenny. You look great! Hi Alex. How are you?" I took her bags and we proceeded to walk to the car.

"I can relax now that you are here. She's been a pest waiting for you." I walked a few steps in front of them, giving them time to talk. Jenny and her aunt had a relationship, deeper than any other aunt and niece relationship I knew. Jenny often said it was because Sally never had a child of her own. I was happy Jenny had Sally to confide in and with whom she could share her accomplishments. Jenny couldn't wait to take her aunt to the school where she volunteered to help struggling students and introduce her to the class. Jenny was very proud of Sally.

Later that night after, Sally gave us the homemade cookies from Jenny's mom and a few thick winter sweaters for Jenny to wear as the days got colder, and we went to dinner. When Jenny went to the restroom, Sally asked me how Jenny was doing being away from home.

"She hasn't complained to me since last fall. She was a little home-sick when she first started here, but then she found great friends and really enjoyed her classes. Jenny is a warm person, so it was easy for her to connect with people and develop friendships, and after a week or two, she found her groove and was on her way."

"I'm glad to hear that. I knew she would thrive out here. You two are great together; you deserve to be happy and should be with each other. Thank you, Alex, for taking special care of her. You know that she means the world to me."

"No need to thank me; she's my world, too."

Jenny

My aunt Sally died suddenly the spring before I graduated from college and I learned I could never let another moment pass me by. I had to jump into life and live. The moment when I stood next to my aunt's casket, I understood people were put on earth with special gifts, and their gifts were meant to be shared with others. Everyone had a purpose, and I was determined to find mine.

After I graduated from college, without classes and tests to focus on, I lost the distraction that kept me from being consumed by the emptiness my aunt had filled in my younger days. Sometimes my job as an assistant teacher didn't offer the diversion I needed. In all honesty, I'd been hiding from my despair over losing my aunt. To escape from my feelings, I started to obsess about getting married. The fact that I would never see my aunt again was too much for me to face. Therefore, instead of trying to accept my life without her and carry on, I created a fantasy and began pressuring Alex to propose to me. Losing myself in daydreams of my wedding day distracted me from feeling that ache inside my heart. I was waiting, not so patiently, for a proposal that it seemed would never come.

By the one-year anniversary of my aunt's death, my emotions and grief after losing her were beginning to heal. I was trying to find myself and ready to take back control of my life. I was growing restless; my destiny was in someone else's hands. Alex wasn't ready to ask me to marry him, and hounding him wasn't going to make it happen any faster. I was not fulfilled working as an assistant teacher, yet I was reminded every day of the happiness Alex had by securing an impressive job as an architect right out of college. The months of pressure I put on Alex to propose didn't produce a ring, so during the day as I moved about the school I started to dream about moving somewhere fresh. I convinced myself if I moved to another state, anywhere but here, it might be easier to find a permanent teaching job, or at least block the memories of my aunt; I was challenged by her memory by staying in the same town she lived in. Maybe someday, I hoped, it would be comforting to see her favorite places, but for now I felt the need to move away while I tried to continue to learn to accept my life without her.

I knew I couldn't put off living my life any longer. I was tired of waiting for something that was out of my control to happen. I loved Alex with all my heart, but at that point in my life I realized I needed to live instead of waiting around to get married.

I wanted to move to the West Coast, where I'd dreamed of living since I was a little girl. I wasn't married, I didn't have kids, and I could easily get a teaching job, or at least become a nanny, in California.

"I'm leaving for California," I told Alex on the Saturday night after the one-year anniversary of my aunt's death. We were at my parents' house, sitting on the couch.

"What? I know you always talked about going there, but moving there — why now?" Alex sounded surprised.

"I'm tired of waiting for my life to start. Every day I find myself thinking, if only I were a full-time teacher or married, I would feel complete. I don't want to be an assistant. I want my own classroom. And, I shouldn't be waiting for a ring, hoping it will change my life. So instead, I'm going to make the change. It's been hard being here without my aunt. I still love you, and I hope maybe you'll come with me." I sat cross-legged, twisting my hair around my finger, something I did when I felt unsure. "But either way, I think I need to do this for me." Staring out the window, I watched the clouds start to move in as the sunlight began to fade. I wasn't sure if I would regret saying what I was thinking—I was being selfish—and then it came out of my mouth. "Sometimes I feel like everything I've done has been for you."

"What! That's a low blow, Jenny. We have done everything for each other. I've given up things for you. I've sacrificed. That's what a relationship is." Alex got off the couch and went to the window. Turning around, he continued. "You can't be serious. How can I get through to you? You can't leave, not now."

I could tell I had made a mistake. I never should have said what I did. He was right—we both had made sacrifices for each other. He gave up his childhood dream of being a professional hockey player when he chose our relationship over signing with a semi-pro team. The years we spent together had changed his views on playing at a professional level. After he graduated from college, he didn't pursue the hockey opportunities that were offered to him. Instead, he chose to go out on top after finishing his most successful season. He knew it would be a challenge to have a relationship and a hockey career; one of them would suffer. He always said, "You only find true love once in a lifetime."

"Listen, Jenny, you've had a hard day. A lot has been going on. Maybe you need a good night's sleep. We can talk more tomorrow." He sat next to me. "Please don't make a hasty decision without talking to me. You'll think clearer after a good sleep." Grabbing his jacket, he kissed me good-bye and said, "Call me when you wake up."

I began to think about moving the day I went shopping for an outfit to wear to my aunt's services, I had run into my high school friend Becky, who had just returned home from LA.

"Jenny, is that you? Oh my goodness, it's been so long." We hugged.

"Hi, Becky. I thought you were living in Los Angeles?"

"I am. Well, I was. I moved back last week. My dad's not feeling well, and my mother needed help running the family business." Becky's family owned the local hardware store, Fix It.

She told me story after story of the fun she had living in LA. The sun-drenched mornings there always seem to become strangled with smog by the afternoon, she said. The winters were easy. I hated winter! She lived with the beach in her backyard, and she would hang at the cool clubs with her friends and co-workers. As I listened to her stories, I couldn't help feeling that I needed to make a change in my life. "Becky, you've done a great job of describing a perfect world, a world I would love to be part of."

I had convinced myself that if I could only get to California, I would be happy. I wouldn't live there forever. I'd stay for a year and see what happened next. If it didn't work out, I knew I could always come back home.

But telling Alex my idea had hurt him. I had seen the hurt I caused in his eyes. The one thing I hadn't thought about in all of this were his feelings. I realized I had a made a mistake. I should have thought it through before telling him. Now I began to have second thoughts about moving. I didn't know what I was thinking. Leaving him and my parents — my parents would die if I moved away. They were still lost in pain and sadness with Sally gone. I loved Alex so much, and I realized I had just hurt him more deeply than I had ever done before. He was my life, and as long as we were together, I was where I wanted and needed to be. The guilt I felt wrenched my gut. How could I have upset him?

I will talk to him tomorrow and tell him I'm not going anywhere. I was a fool to think I needed to move to California to be happy.

Alex

ON THE DRIVE HOME, IF MY HANDS HAD GRIPPED THE STEERING wheel any harder I would have snapped it in two. The windows were down; I hoped the fresh night air would help clear my mind. I was trying to understand what had just happened. How could she pull this now? I had made the choice to live at home instead of moving in with friends, so I could save chunks of my paycheck to buy her a diamond. Sally's death had caused the family to adjust their lives and learn to live without her. In Jenny's opinion, planning for her wedding would take away her grief and give her mother something positive to think about. It was all she had talked about for the last year. And now I had the ring, she told me she is planning to move to California.

I drove around the bend in the road and thought about how my childhood dreams of following in my grandfather's footsteps as a hockey pro hadn't happened, but I did follow my father's path by studying architecture and engineering in college. I pursued my love of art and design, and I secured a job with help from my father. It was ideal that he owned his own highly successful engineering firm. Having a job in the field I enjoyed encouraged me to continue with more education. After a one-year break from college, I planned to return to night school in the fall. After three years I would receive my master's degree, which would give me an edge over the competition.

Over the last three months, I tried to explain to Jenny that I didn't want to get married until I was finished with school. I told her I didn't want any big life changes or distractions while in school and convinced her that earning a master's degree would set us up for a better life. But all I ever wanted was to make Jenny happy, so I made the decision to propose now, knowing we could have a long engagement. I would be busy working and going to school, giving Jenny plenty of time to dream about and plan our wedding.

I arrived home and parked in my parents' driveway. In my bedroom, I felt my stomach tighten as I opened the nightstand drawer and reached in and pulled out the little black velvet box. The creaking noise it made when I opened it reminded me of the sound my heart made when Jenny told me she wanted to move. Holding the sparkling new diamond between my fingers, I wondered, *Is this what it will take to get her to stay?* I stared at the sparkling facets and pondered whether I should continue with my plans for tomorrow. I didn't want Jenny to think I only asked her to get married to convince her to stay, but I had to do something. I fell asleep holding onto my only chance of keeping the girl I loved.

Most of my dreams that night were of falling. My arms reached out, flailing around, trying to grasp something; people were laughing, smiling, and pointing. I couldn't figure it out. I tossed and turned. What did it all mean? And then, there she was, Jenny, looking beautiful and peaceful in a long, flowing white dress, her delicate feet peeking out from underneath. She looked as pretty as an angel. But when I reached out my hand to her, she disappeared. I had seen her and felt her love, and then she was gone—not instantly though. Her image gradually faded, and then she disappeared. I woke immediately and sat up, breathing hard, soaked in sweat. She was my angel; I believed that. *She's saved me from making many mistakes, and I couldn't let her disappear from my life.* I knew what I had to do.

Jenny

THE SUNLIGHT FILTERED THROUGH MY CURTAINS. I COULD HEAR the birds chirping through my open window, and the fragrant smell of springtime washed over me as I stretched my arms over my head. My thoughts rushed to Alex. *How is he feeling after our conversation last night?* I needed to talk to him.

I felt sick to my stomach, and I hoped breakfast would help me feel better. I headed downstairs to the kitchen. My father sat at the table. "Good morning, sunshine!"

"Hi, Dad," I replied as I walked to the coffee maker.

"I wouldn't touch that. Alex should be here any time now with your breakfast."

"Alex?" My stomachache deepened. "What do you mean?" I turned around.

"He called a little while ago and said not to let you eat, because he was bringing you breakfast. I thought you would have heard the phone."

I smiled at my dad. I shouldn't have doubted Alex. He always knew how to make me feel good.

Gracie barked when the door opened. "It's just me," I heard Alex remark to the dog.

As he came around the corner I couldn't help but notice how handsome he was in his white t-shirt and jeans. Watching Alex's body change from the teenager I fell in love with to the man he was today proved how long we had been with each other.

I walked over to him, looked up into his eyes, and felt my stomach flutter. He slipped his empty arm around my waist, pulled me in tight, and whispered in my ear, "I have a surprise for you." From behind his back he pulled out a huge bouquet of flowers. I stood, speechless, staring at the beautiful flower arrangement in his hand.

"Roses, my favorite. They smell amazing!" I lit up, smiling from ear to ear, and suddenly my stomachache was gone.

"That's just the reaction I was hoping for, Jenny." He kissed my cheek. "I have another surprise. Meet me out on the patio, okay?"

"I'll put these in a vase and be right out."

I was sitting on the patio in the warm morning sunshine when Alex walked out with a bag and two coffees. I smiled at him as he opened the bag and handed me a bagel. We sat alone on the patio eating the bagels and drinking coffee. Alex brought up LA first.

"So, Jenny, I thought about what you said about moving. I know how you feel about wanting to get on with life, but I don't see how moving is going to fulfill you." He took a bite of his bagel and looked at me, waiting patiently for me to answer.

"Alex, I think I spoke too soon. I've been emotional since my aunt died. I got caught up in the stories Becky told me. I was thinking about it after you left last night. You're right, yesterday was an emotional day after a long week of preparing for Aunt Sally's service. I was tired and looking for an escape from life." I took a sip of coffee. "Becky's stories made it sound like LA was the life I wanted, but it's not what I want. I know that now. I always dreamed about moving out west and how magical it would be, but after you left I thought more about it. I realized it doesn't always end up the way you think it will. I don't want to hurt you or break your heart. You're more important to me than moving anywhere. I love you, Alex."

"I'm relieved to hear you say that." He took my hand in his, looked me in the eye, and told me, "Wherever you chose to go, I will be by your side. But I believe we are meant to be here, not in LA."

"Sometimes situations happen. People say things they don't always mean, but they need to hear themselves say it out loud. That's what happened to me last night. After I said it, it didn't feel right. Alex, I don't think I'm meant to be in LA. I'm meant to be here with you." I held his hand and felt the strength in it. I knew he could provide me the strength I needed to heal from Aunt Sally's death.

"Then I'll continue with my plan after all."

I looked at him with a puzzled expression. "What does that mean?"

"You'll have to wait and see." He winked at me as he took a sip of coffee.

Alex

I HAD PLANNED A SURPRISE FOR JENNY THAT WEEKEND, AND I WAS not going to let her confusion about moving to California stop me.

As we finished our breakfast, I said, "I was thinking we should have a cookout tonight with our families. Maybe it would help distract your parents from the emotions they are feeling over Sally's anniversary."

"Yeah, that sounds nice. The weather is perfect. I'm sure my mother wouldn't mind. She enjoys your parents' company. Having everyone together, she'll feel loved."

I pushed the grocery cart around the store as Jenny tossed food in. I wondered how many people Jenny planned to feed — we'd invited our families, not the neighborhood. My parents and my sister and her boyfriend were coming, along with Jenny's parents and her brother and his wife.

Jenny's father, Bob, was the only person who knew of my plan. He'd told me he was more than happy to help out, and he planned to work around the yard all day, keeping my secret safe. As I thought about Bob in the yard, setting up for the cookout and acting as the event planner, I tried to keep my excitement under control. I had planned everything, from Jenny's favorite flowers to our love songs. Bob was overjoyed to help me orchestrate a perfect evening for Jenny.

I followed Jenny upstairs when she went to get ready for the cookout. I wanted to make sure she wore the right outfit to celebrate a night she would never forget. Tonight would be a lasting memory, one that she could relive in her mind over and over again. She looked through her closet and started taking out skirts and t-shirts, not the right clothes for what I had in store for her. I knew she would want to be dressed up for this night. I held up a perfect salmon-colored cocktail dress. "Will you wear this dress for me, Jenny?"

She turned to me and said with a sassy attitude, "Since when do you pick out my outfits?"

I felt like I needed to cover up any clues about the surprise, so, trying to play it cool, I told her, "I love the way you look in this. It reminds me of last summer. Remember, we danced all night long at your cousin's wedding?"

She looked the dress over. "I recall a lot more than just dancing with you in this dress," she said with a wink. "Okay, I'll wear if it will make you happy. I like this dress, and it looks good on me."

Jenny came downstairs as the guests arrived. When she walked out the French doors in the back of the house, she noticed that her back yard had been transformed into a magical place. I heard her ask her father as he lit the last of the candles, "Dad, what happened here?"

"I felt like putting some extra touches to the night. Don't you look beautiful!" He leaned in and kissed her cheek.

I stood in the shadows underneath the canopy of a tree in the back corner, watching Jenny take in the enchanting decorations. Tiki torches lit the path to the patio; lanterns flickering rays of candlelight hung from tree branches; the tables were covered in white tablecloths set with vases full of dense pink, cream, and purple flower arrangements. Votive candles twinkled atop the circular tables. When she heard the music coming from the speakers, she smiled. "Wonderful Tonight" by Eric Clapton played softly.

"Dad, this isn't right. It seems more like a party than a cookout." She turned to find her father has disappeared.

She turned again when she heard my feet crunch the stones as I walked up the lit path toward her, my hair still wet from my shower. She spun in a slow circle, looking at all the decorations, and I felt lucky to observe the expression on Jenny's face as she took in the beauty that surrounded her.

"What do you think, Jenny? This is all for you, love." I planted a tender kiss on her cheek and held her hand.

"I don't understand what's happening; I thought we were having a cookout, not a party. This place looks amazing. What are you up to?"

I led her by her hand past the tiki torches; we walked to the patio as the song changed. Louie Armstrong sang about birds and trees and red roses. I took her in my arms for just a moment and then spun her out and back into my embrace. Her eyes sparkled. Speechless, she looked at me, her mouth turned up just a bit at the corners.

I spoke as we moved to the music.

Looking down into her eyes, I told her, "Jenny, I have loved you since the first time I saw you. Having you in my life has made me complete, and I know my life without you would be empty. Every decision I need to make, I keep you in mind. When I look in your eyes I see someone full of love and full of life. Jenny, I love you so much. You're the only one I want to see when I wake up, and I want you to be the last one I see before shutting my eyes. The years that we've been together have been the best years of my life." I released her arms, dropped to one knee, and looked up into her striking eyes before continuing. "We've taken it slow enough. Jenny, will you marry me?"

She smiled down at me but didn't speak. Her eyes searched my face, and I wondered if she'd heard me. I knew she had dreamed of this day since she was a little girl. She had once told me about the fantasy she had of flowers, candles, and love songs. Her smile expanded, and I saw tears fill in her eyes. As a tear fell from her eye, she spoke, wiping the tears away with her fingertip. "Yes. Yes, I want nothing more than to marry you, Alex."

I stood, and she hugged me so hard I could barely breathe. I couldn't pry her arms from my neck, so I asked her to let go for a minute. "Let me do this right." I got on one knee again, and I opened the black velvet box. Looking up, I asked, "Jenny Ann Parker, will you marry me?"

She held out her left hand, and I placed the engagement ring on her ring finger. "Yes, I will, Alex Patrick Murphy."

Jenny

OUR WEDDING WAS HELD ON THE AFTERNOON OF THE TWELFTH of June, one of the most magical days of our lives. We had planned an outside reception. The sun pushed the clouds from the sky and radiated warmth to the ground. Alex enjoyed a golf outing in the morning with his dad and friends. I spent my last morning as a single woman at the spa with my mother and bridesmaids. We talked about how much things had changed; we hoped our relationships would stay strong. I doubted Alex's morning was as deeply emotional as mine.

Alex and I spoke on the phone before we left for our morning celebrations with our friends and families. I was filled with anticipation, and I needed to hear his voice and share how excited I was that our wedding day had finally arrived. I hoped he would help calm my nerves.

As the phone rang before connecting me to him, my heart raced with every ring tone. When he answered the phone, my nerves settled at the sound of his voice.

"Hello?"

"Hi, Alex. I'm so excited that I had to call you. I can't believe the day is here." I couldn't contain my enthusiasm.

"I know — it feels like it came so fast! Just think — by the end of today, you will officially be Jenny Ann Murphy, my wife."

"Yeah, and you'll still be Alex Patrick Murphy, but you'll be my husband." He laughed.

"I'll see you at the altar. I love you, Alex."

"I'll be the guy in the black tux waiting for you. Don't make me wait long. I love you too, Jenny."

Later I stood at the back of the church with my dad as the bridal party proceeded down the aisle. All the bridesmaids wore lilac dresses and carried flower bouquets in mixtures of pink and purple. When it was my turn to walk through the doors, I heard everyone gasp. My father leaned over and told me I looked spectacular. I was wearing a gown made of a soft white silk under a sheer overlay; delicate hand-stitched silk flowers flowed over the sheer bodice. I wore my hair up in a classic style. My veil was attached with a small tiara covered in pearls. I carried a huge bouquet of pink roses with stems wrapped in a silk ribbon. My mother was with me when I found my dress. I'd tried on ten different styles, but I knew the first one I saw would be the one I loved most.

As my father and I made our way down the aisle, I couldn't take my eyes off Alex. He was the most beautiful groom I had ever seen. His tuxedo made him look like a true gentleman. With his freshly trimmed hair, he looked polished, like a model. My anticipation grew with every step my father and I took that closed the gap to Alex. After what felt like a mile, I finally stood next to him. Before walking away, my father placed my hand in Alex's, and I heard him say to Alex, "Take good care of her." Alex replied, "I will, sir." Alex wore a huge smile and had a twinkle in his eye.

Then he turned to me and whispered in my ear, "You look beautiful." I got lost looking up into Alex's eyes. The moment before there had been a church full of people; now all I saw was Alex standing in front of me. I always felt a sense of completeness being with him; I didn't need to be anywhere else. If I'd had any worries that day, they disappeared when I stood next to him.

After we exchanged our vows, "in good times and in bad, in sickness and in health, 'til death do us part," the priest officially declared us husband and wife. Alex held my hands in his, and we shared our first kiss as Mr. and Mrs. Alex Murphy. All my dreams were coming true.

At the reception, everyone gathered around us as we danced to our first song as a married couple, "The Way You Look Tonight" — Alex's choice. We had debated over too many songs we both loved. All night long we danced and we laughed, celebrating love with friends and family. It seemed everyone could feel our energy, and it spread joy to everyone there.

By the end of the night, we were tired and looking forward to our honeymoon in Bermuda. The wedding planning had been more work than we thought it would be. A vacation together was in order.

Jenny

"GOOD MORNING, MRS. MURPHY." ALEX WAS PROPPED ON HIS elbow staring at me when I opened my eyes to the new day.

"Good morning." I was groggy, and my voice reflected that. I stretched my arms above my head and rolled over to kiss him before he climbed out of the bed.

"In a few hours we will be starting a week of fun in the sun. I can't wait to get there. Out of bed, lazy bones — we have a plane to catch." Alex whipped the sheets off me.

After a short plane ride, a taxi drove us to our hotel. Alex opened the door to our oceanfront honeymoon suite. I was drawn to the slider and opened it. I walked out onto the balcony that overlooked the swimming pool and the blue ocean with white-capped waves that would be our back yard for the next week. As I inhaled the sea air, every muscle in my body released. I was on my honeymoon.

"Just as they promised. Look at this view!" Warmed by the sun's rays, I looked out over the picturesque Caribbean scenery. Alex came up behind me. I turned around to look him in the eye.

Holding me around my waist, he asked, "What are we going to do first, Mrs. Murphy?"

I was so excited to be on vacation at the beach, I felt like a little kid. I couldn't wait to put on my bathing suit and go jump in the waves. "Did you look at the view? Look at the beach and the ocean."

I noticed Alex was studying my body in my cotton candy pink sundress. I sensed he had other things on his mind.

"I'm sorry. How can I look anywhere else when we're finally alone and you're wearing that hot dress?" He wrapped his arms tighter around my body. "Yes, that's a great view. We'll go play at the beach a little later, but now I want to see what is under this dress."

As he lifted the dress over my head, I was swept away from the beach and into Alex's feelings. Certainly a little romp in between the sheets wouldn't hurt anything. He was eyeing my body, and it seemed he liked what he saw. He took my face in his hands and gently placed a kiss on my lips. He pulled back and looked into my eyes. "I love you," he said, and before I could answer, his lips were kissing me again, this time with more passion. I returned his kiss. It sent a shockwave of love from head to toe. Alex kissed his way down my neck to my chest. Stopping for only a second, he unfastened my strapless bra; it fell to the floor. He found my nipple with his tongue; it hardened when his warm, wet tongue tickled it, and I let out a slight moan. He laid me on my back and continued to kiss my skin, moving slowly over the areas that he knew would excite me. When he finished kissing every inch of my body, he returned to my lips.

"Are you enjoying yourself?"

"Um, yes, very much." I grabbed his waist, unfastening the button on his shorts. "Maybe it is better I show you instead of telling you." I winked at him.

"Oh, I like the sound of that." He kissed my cheek.

"Good, now let's have some more fun." I took off his clothes. When I finished pleasing him, he got on top of me, and I felt him enter. Our bodies moved in rhythm; every push he made sent waves of emotions through my body, I was aroused by his movements. We made love all afternoon. I had never before felt what I felt that day. I experienced eternal bliss.

Our honeymoon was a week filled with love and laughter. We recalled the memories of the wedding, all the nerves and the anticipation. We both agreed it was a day we would never forget and relished

in the thoughts of continuing our lives together side by side, through
thick and thin.

Jenny

OUR LIVES TOGETHER STARTED OUT THE WAY I'D HOPED. SHORTLY after returning from our honeymoon, we found a parcel of land to build a home on. It had been Alex's childhood dream to design a home to raise a family in. We noticed the development that would become Steeple Circle when we took a weekend ride to see the newer developments that were beginning to take over the forests and farm-land. Most of the lots at the beginning of the development were still available; only one was still available at the end of the circle, and we fell in love with the lot and the street, knowing that our future children could run and ride their bikes safely. My heart and soul were filled, and all my dreams were coming true.

We bought the land in the new development and continued to live in our one-bedroom apartment to save money, so we could afford to build the dream house Alex had envisioned when he was younger. We often drove out to look at the land. On one visit, I noticed growing activity on the lot next to ours. The peace that surrounded Steeple Circle was broken when a family began building their house next to our vacant lot. I was excited about the new neighbors, and I prayed for a young family that would complement mine. And that's just what we got.

I took a full-time position teaching second grade at the school where I'd worked as an assistant teacher. I would start in September alongside all the nervous students beginning their school year. I was thrilled to have my own classroom where I would teach students how to write stories and build their mathematics skills. All the hard work I put into my career was paying off. I looked forward to a satisfying career and a long life with Alex.

Three years into our marriage, the dream house was still not complete. We had moved through the process slowly. Alex needed to finish designing the house and then mentally live in it, picturing himself in every room and correcting any flaws before deciding it was ready to be built.

As he was achieving his dreams of building a home, I was dreaming of the family we would raise in it. I was ready, at peace with the idea of a little baby coming into our lives. Alex struggled with the notion; he wanted to make sure our lives were in order before becoming a dad. We agreed to start trying, knowing it could take time to conceive, but we didn't have long to organize our lives. We got pregnant the first time we tried.

I was unsure of how Alex would react to the news. Not wanting him to diminish the joy I felt, I decided to leave the pregnancy test for him in his work bag alongside a note:

> *Dear Alex,*
>
> *Surprise, Daddy! I can only hope you are as excited as me. All our love and dreams will grow with the new baby. Thank you for making me a mother.*
>
> *Your loving wife,*
> *Jenny*

I heard Alex come in the door as I was finishing dinner in our cozy galley kitchen.

"Hi, honey," I called from the kitchen.

"Hi, Mommy." Alex hugged me. "I got your letter. Fine way of telling me! I've been a wreck all day. I wasn't sure if I should tell people or not. I wanted to call you, but I was in meetings most of the day." He sounded upset. "Jenny, I wish you told me face to face."

"I wanted you to have time to think about it. I wasn't sure I could handle your reaction if you weren't as excited as me." I raised my brows, waiting anxiously to hear what he would say.

"Honestly, I'm a little shocked. I thought you said it would take months. I wasn't expecting to be a father this fast. There are still things that need to be done."

"Well, now you have nine months to finish them." I planted a kiss on his lips and held up a cold beer for him.

"Thanks, I need that. The beer *and* the nine months." He smiled at me, and I chuckled.

Jenny

"DEEP BREATH AND PUSH! YOU CAN DO IT, JENNY. THE BABY IS almost out," Alex cheered me on.

The pregnancy went by so fast that in some ways I felt like I'd just found out I was pregnant and then I was in labor. The pregnancy was challenging at first; every day began with my head in the toilet. As the months passed the nausea went away, and I enjoyed the fluttering feelings of the baby swimming around in its own pool. Alex was a great father-in-training, always up to the task of a foot rub or running out for ice cream, I tried not to ask for too much from him. I would wait for the baby to arrive before I would do that.

My contractions started late at night. Perhaps the Fourth of July fireworks helped get them started. We got to the hospital at seven in the morning, and by noon we were minutes away from seeing and holding our new baby.

I looked up into the doctor's eyes. "Jenny, with the next push, the baby will be out. On your next contraction, take a big inhale, bear down, and push. Push against the contraction. You can do it—you're almost there."

I felt the contraction overtake me and tighten around my stomach. I stared at the doctor, took a big breath, closed my eyes, and pushed. I felt a lot pressure and then a release—it was over. The baby was crying, the cord wrapped all around it. I couldn't see if it was a boy or a girl.

I anxiously waited for the doctor to tell us what the baby was.

"It's a boy. Congratulations, Jenny and Alex. Jenny, you were amazing. You're a strong girl. Alex, you were a loving devoted coach." The doctor placed the baby on my stomach. His body was so tiny, and his arms and legs were stretched out, flailing around. I looked up at Alex and started to cry.

As I held our newborn baby in my arms, I was awestruck by his perfection and enjoyed the sweet grunting noises he made. I looked up to see that Alex, the man I was in love with, was crying. He had a tender heart and was not ashamed of his emotions, one of the many things I loved about him. When I stared into the baby's eyes and held his tiny fist in my hand, I recalled how Alex and I got here, all the years we had spent building our relationship and designing a home to raise our family in. I handed our new baby boy to Alex and I thought, *Now we're a family. Alex, Jenny, and baby Nicolas.*

"Jenny, he's perfect, a blend of you and me. I can't believe our love made this little guy." He stared at his new son with admiration. "We have to share him with our parents — they'll love him." Alex couldn't take his eyes off his new baby boy.

"He's a gift from God," I said as Alex admired his son's face.

"So you say, but I believe we had something to do with it too," he said in reply, taking credit for his part in creating his son.

I looked at Alex holding our son in his loving embrace, thinking I wouldn't have wanted to share this with anyone but Alex. After the support and love he showed me during the pregnancy, I was certain he was going to be a great father. He'd come with me to every doctor's appointment, and he was patient with me during every hormonally charged emotional outburst. I think he knew it wasn't wise to fight with a pregnant woman. Watching Alex hold our son reminded me of sitting around when I was younger, dreaming of the day I would become a mother and have my own family. That day had arrived.

Alex

MY EMOTIONS WERE RICH, AND I FELT ALIVE AS I HELD MY newborn son in my arms. He was a real expression of my love for Jenny. I was so proud of her strength to endure labor to bring our son into this world.

I was a father. As I held Nicolas for the first time, I dreamed of watching him grow into a young boy. It seemed impossible that the tiny baby in my arms would grow up to throw baseballs and pedal a bike. The magnitude of love I had for Jenny was doubled for Nicolas; my parental instincts kicked in, and I was prepared to protect him from any harm. I now understood my parents' reactions when life wasn't kind to me. As a new parent, I had a different appreciation for the desire to keep children safe and happy.

I watched Jenny navigate through her first days as a mother. We were both nervous with every cry Nicolas let out. We ran through the checklist of baby demands: hunger, wet diaper, upset tummy, over-stimulation, being tired. At some point we would hit on the demand that Nicolas was making, and peace would be restored to the house.

Days following Nicolas' birth, the vibrant energy Jenny once had slowly began to disappear, and I worried about her attitude toward life. I knew her body was responding to the pregnancy hormones. My guy friends reassured me that their wives had suffered the same fate and that it would pass.

I wished Jenny could have appreciated Nicolas in the first months the way I did. He was a miracle that our love created; wrapped in flesh and bones, with a beating heart. I was always in awe when I looked at him; he came into our lives through our love and connected Jenny to me more than anything else could.

Although Jenny lacked the happiness I expected her to feel about being a new mother, she had a natural way with Nicolas that I lacked. Nicolas seemed to fit in her arms very comfortably, like a baby bird in a nest. When I held him and fumbled around to get him in a comfortable position, I worried I would drop him, and when he was content my muscles relaxed with relief. But before I knew it, something happened. The phone rang, I sneezed, or he would squirm, and I would have to start over again. Jenny encouraged me and said that as Nicolas grew, it would be easier for me to hold him. I looked forward to that day, but I wasn't in any hurry to get there.

When I returned to work three weeks after his birth, I worried about leaving Jenny alone. She enjoyed teaching for eight years, but decided not to return after Nicolas' birth. My days with Nicolas in my life were busier. I would finish work and rush home to relieve Jenny from her mothering responsibilities, hoping it would help her cope with her new lifestyle. She was quick to hand Nicolas over and take care of whatever she needed to, whether it was reading to relax or taking a ride or going for a walk—anything to get out of the apartment. I kept a watchful eye on her for many months and was reassured when she finally revealed happier moments of joy; she was growing into her new role as a mother.

Having a family and being able to build a house to share with my loved ones thrilled me. I got a lot of satisfaction from manipulating the structural layout of the design; the improvements I had made in the designs for the new house were almost complete. When I studied the blueprints, I envisioned me and my family moving from one room to the next; I kept in mind the flow and movement we would need to get from one room to another. With Nicolas' birth, I had reason to work faster to complete the design and move forward in the process of building our family home.

Jenny

TROUBLE STARTED A FEW DAYS AFTER WE CAME HOME FROM THE hospital. At first, I dismissed my moods as a result of raging hormones and lack of sleep that would cloud anyone's mind. However, my feelings grew darker. One day I thought my world would come to an end. I couldn't get out of bed, and my brain was in a fog. I never dreamed I would suffer from postpartum depression, but as the days and nights merged together as endless, flowing time, I was discovering the truth. As the weeks passed, tidal waves of emotions controlled my day. I kept thinking it would get better when Nicolas slept more, but that wasn't happening.

How could it be that what I'd wanted so badly was torturing me? No one had prepared me for it; I had fooled myself to think by waiting to have a baby until I was in my thirties, and being more mature I would be better prepared for the sudden change. Alex supported me the best he could, but it wasn't enough to soothe my insecurities over being a new mother. As soon as Alex came home from work, he took Nicolas and gave me a break to rest. Knowing that I had Alex's love and support helped get me through my days, a constant reminder of why I'd wanted to have a family with him. As always, he was the one to make it better.

My alone time after Alex came home helped me to realize I was still myself deep down inside, but my life was different now. Knowing Alex was taking care of Nicolas, I was able to do things for myself, like go for walks, which allowed me to focus on how I was feeling. I realized I would have to work hard every day to remind myself that these thoughts and feelings would pass. I taped positive quotes around the apartment to remind myself to have good, uplifting thoughts. I spent more time praying and meditating. I knew the power of prayer. My grandmother had taught me when I was younger, and she would always say to me, "When in doubt, pray it out." Prayer was one thing I could never share with Alex. No matter how I tried, I could not convince him that praying could change his life. Someday he would be ready to believe in the power of prayer. I knew it would happen for him in his own way, like it did for everyone.

In meditation and prayer, I shared my thoughts and feelings with God, and I felt a lightness begin to build. As the weeks turned into months I felt my energy changing. I was able to follow a schedule with Nicolas knowing how each day would unfold, and feeling more in control. Our days started with breakfast, followed by a brisk walk around the neighborhood. He napped while I showered. After lunch we did errands or met friends to pass the afternoon. As my life began to fall into a routine again, my emotions became more balanced and I was able to focus on the many blessings in my life.

By the time Nicolas reached his first birthday, I was enjoying my role as his mother. As I rocked him to sleep on the night of his first birthday, the anniversary of the day that created a change in me, I realized having him in my life had forced me to grow more than anything else could have. I survived my bout with postpartum depression and was later able to help friends who suffered the same fate. The comfort that arose from knowing who I was because of what I had been through made my suffering worth it. I now had the ability to look at my life and realize what I could change and learn to accept what I couldn't. Nicolas caused a profound stir in me. He taught me that I wasn't in control of everything, but if I had faith, I could get through anything.

Alex

I TOOK THE CALL JUST BEFORE LUNCH. JENNY INFORMED ME THE house inspection was placed on hold because the electrician hadn't wired the smoke detectors properly, so the fire department prohibited us from moving in. When I called the electrician, his receptionist told me he was on vacation and wouldn't be available to make the necessary changes for a couple of weeks.

After Nicolas was in bed later that night, I told Jenny about my frustrations.

"I can't believe this. We hire this guy, who we picked over the other three who bid the job and he can't even do the job right. So, because of his incompetence we can't move in this weekend and have to wait for him to come home and find time to fix it." I was furious.

"Alex, I know you're upset. I am, too, but maybe this a sign."

I interrupted. "Oh, here we go again with your *signs*." I headed for the kitchen, and Jenny followed.

"I know you don't believe in signs and spirits, and there's no way I could convince you to pray about it, but I really think this electrician issue could be keeping us safe from something we don't even know about."

I fixed a snack while Jenny sat at the small table that was crammed in the corner of our tiny kitchen. "Remember a few months ago, when I left the apartment and forgot my wallet?" she said. "I went back to get it, and only later did I find out that there had been a bad accident on the same road I was traveling just minutes after I turned around."

I smirked to show I didn't believe a higher power had intervened in her life that day.

"Jenny, there is nothing out there controlling your behavior and events in your life. We are in control of our own destiny. I had control over everything and everyone on this project. I had them lined up to finish their work on time, so that we could move in this weekend. And now because some buffoon didn't check his work, we have to suffer." I slammed the refrigerator door shut.

"Alex, please, calm down. It will be fine. I don't mind waiting, and Nicolas is only two. He doesn't know the difference between an apartment and a new house. There's a bigger plan here. We can't see it, but we need to trust in it."

"You can trust in it, but as for me, I am taking back control. I'll find another electrician, one that's more capable than the one we hired. I'll make sure we are in by at least the middle of next week. I want to be in before October."

"I wish you could have faith that this will work out and see how irrationally you are acting. You are not in control of everything in your life. Things like this have a way of working themselves out.

"I do believe that this will work itself out. I'm going to help it along. You can't always sit back in life, Jenny, and expect the *spirits* to do the work for you."

"I know that, Alex, but maybe you shouldn't push so hard. You could learn to accept things in life that go against what you think you want and have faith that you will get exactly what you need."

"My mother tried to teach me that life lesson, and it didn't work. She tried praying with me and telling me to talk to God about problems I had, but it never worked for me. I never got what I wanted."

Nicolas's crying carried through the apartment. Jenny got up from the table, and as she left the room, she turned to say, "God doesn't give you what you want, Alex. He gives you what you need. I hope someday you will discover that."

Jenny

MONTHS AFTER NICOLAS TURNED TWO, WE'D NO SOONER HAM-
mered the last nail into the house on Steeple Circle than I discovered
that our many months of attempting to conceive again were finally
successful. The saying is true: "a new house and a new baby." This
time I surprised Alex with the news by writing baby number two's
room on one of the boxes for the spare room. I asked him to help me
carry the box into the bedroom and then asked him to open it. Alex
nearly fell over when he saw the pregnancy test sitting on top of Nicolas's crib bedding.

"What's this? Jenny, are you pregnant again?" He looked like he
was seeing a ghost.

I nodded and smiled. "Are you okay, Alex?"

"I'm okay. I just wasn't expecting it—you caught me by surprise.
Man, you are good at surprises. Come here, Mommy." He held me in
his arms and said, "This is why we have this house, so we can fill it with
little Murphys. I'm so excited, Jenny."

Our new house was more beautiful than the visual images I imagined from the blueprints Alex designed. Every room was purposefully
laid out to support how our family would use the house. The kitchen
and family room were placed in the back of the house; they were the
largest rooms on the first floor, offering plenty of space to entertain
and enjoy our guests and family. Like most houses, the dining and
living rooms were located in the front. The children's bedrooms were
painted in their favorite colors, blue and yellow. I loved spending time

in my kitchen, but our master bedroom was the true design master-piece, with special lighting, walk-in closets and a dream bathroom that I never wanted to leave. The design offered me enough space to decorate the room as a bedroom and a sitting room; and during the planning stage I often dreamt of retreating there for a mommy time-out.

My favorite part of having the house complete was watching Alex lead the tour for our family and friends or the neighbors. He wore a proud smile and held his posture like a lion walking around his pride. He enjoyed the compliments from the guests as they explored the house and took note of the details in Alex's workmanship. While Alex was a phenomenal hockey player, his ability to create a design for a house or a building was just as impressive, and he enjoyed the recognition he received.

As we were moving into our house, we met many of our new neighbors: the Hills and McCarthys lived at the beginning of the development; the Lees and Russos lived opposite each other. Our house was next to the Sullivan's house at the end of the cul-de-sac. The Sullivans had often come over as our house was being built to offer the use of their bathroom. Sometimes they helped to keep Nicolas occupied while Alex and I checked on the progress the builders were making. Having Ben and Julie Sullivan for neighbors was a gift; they were the only ones who had a child, Mathew, the same age as Nicolas.

I knew after the first time I met Julie Sullivan that we would grow to have a close friendship. We made an instant connection. We were so alike — she was the blond version of me. After we settled in, we spent most days at each other's homes. The boys were thrilled to have one another to play with.

One morning a couple months after we moved in, Julie was bringing Mathew over to play with Nicolas. When she knocked on the door that led into the house from the garage, I was in the bathroom, just on the other side of the door, dry heaving. Julie opened the unlocked door and called out, "Jenny, is everything okay?"

I flushed the toilet and walked out of the bathroom to face Julie. I must have looked rather green.

"Hi, Julie. Don't worry—I don't have the flu. Come into the kitchen. I need a glass of water." She followed behind and told Mathew to go find Nicolas.

"Jenny, what's going on? Is everything okay?" She took a seat at the island as I poured two glasses of water. The morning sun lit-up my new kitchen drowning it in warmth. I was thrilled to have a larger kitchen in which to entertain.

"Believe it or not, I couldn't be happier. I wasn't planning on telling anyone this soon, but I found out a couple months ago I'm pregnant." The smile on my face was so big it forced color back into my cheeks.

"Oh my, Jenny. You're not going to believe this—I'm pregnant too. We found out last month. I've been waiting till I get closer to the twelve-week mark to say anything." She walked over and wrapped me in her arms. "I'm sorry you're not feeling well. It should pass."

"I can't believe this! This is going to be great. Oh, I hope they are the same sex—that will make things so much easier," I said, thankful for Julie.

"I'm praying for a girl," Julie said. "Well, I want a healthy baby, but I also pray the healthy baby is a girl." We laughed and sat in silence for a moment. I was envisioning the years our families would spend together, watching our children grow, helping each other through the challenges of raising children. Julie broke the silence, "I'm blessed to have you in my life, Jenny."

About nine months after we moved into our dream home, we welcomed the daughter we named Jessica into our lives, and a month later, Julie and Ben welcomed baby Annie. The changes after the new baby didn't have the same deep effect as when I had Nicolas. This time I felt a little more prepared for the journey. We quickly fell into the new rhythm of our lives, and I enjoyed being in our new, larger home with the kids. I had places to go if I needed a mommy time-out.

Over the years, Julie and I became more like sisters than friends. We often remarked how similar we were. We both enjoyed running and practicing yoga, and we both had an addiction to coffee. We found that out one day when Julie ran out and came banging on my front door early that morning for a cup from my kitchen. "I just need a cup to get me going. It's my fuel." We laughed that coffee was a sub-urban drug of choice for mothers. As more time went by, we discov-ered our shared love for reading and the joy we felt from going to the movies on a rainy day. We both dearly loved our children, but more than anything, we each had a deep love and appreciation for our hus-bands. While many of our other friends seemed to tolerate their hus-bands, whose existence seemed to be about providing for their mate-rial needs, it was different for Julie and me. We had strong marriages that were a product of mutual respect and desire to grow together.

Jenny

WHEN BEN'S FATHER HAD TO BE RUSHED TO THE HOSPITAL WITH chest pains, Julie asked me to watch her children. Julie told me later that she got to the hospital after Ben did and found him and his mother in the waiting room of the ICU. His sister was out of town on business, they kept her informed through phone calls.

They discovered Ben's dad had a small blockage that led to a heart attack. It was a warning that saved his life. After many tests, a shunt was put in. He was monitored for months and received positive results. He was able to resume his active life style but became more aware of the special moments in each new day.

About a year later, Julie shared her concerns about a report she'd seen on television regarding heart disease; I encouraged her to talk to Ben. A few days later, she talked to Ben when they were getting ready for bed.

"I was watching the news earlier today. They had a special health report on men's heart disease. Have you ever thought about having a stress test to see how healthy your heart is? Maybe your father's heart attack was a warning for you to take better care of yourself."

He rinsed his mouth with water and turned to face her. "Julie, I know what happened to my father last year scared you and whatever you saw on television today reinforced it, but I'm a healthy guy. You have nothing to worry about."

"Ben, I think it wouldn't be a bad idea to look into it. You're not as active as you used to be, you're traveling more for work, and the added stress of providing for our family weighs on you. Plus the fact that your father has had a heart attack—these are indicators that you should be aware of the condition of your heart. If for no other reason, consider doing it for the kids. They deserve to have their father around to watch them grew up."

He kissed the tip of her nose. "If you feel that strongly about it, I'll call the doctor and see what I should do."

But Ben kept putting it off. Many months passed, and as summer faded into fall, she continued to hound Ben to call the doctor. Every time, he had an excuse about why he couldn't make an appointment. Either he was too busy during the day to take time off, or he forgot to call before the office closed, or he was certain his heart was fine. But when she threatened to call for him, he said he would call the next day. She told me she was relieved when she heard him leaving himself a voicemail at his office to remind him to call the doctor.

The next night when they were cleaning up from dinner and the kids were finishing a movie, he told her he'd called the doctor, but they couldn't fit him in for two months. "I guess he's really backed up. The receptionist told me she'd put me on a cancellation list and call with his first opening."

Julie described opening her arms for a hug, satisfied he'd at least reached out to the doctor. "Thank you for calling him."

"You're welcome. Now will you stop nagging me?" he said with laughter in his voice.

"I'll never stop nagging you." She kissed his cheek before walking away to put the leftovers in the refrigerator.

Julie and I shared a pot of coffee for the first time in more than a week; the kids played around the house, and in between interruptions from the kids, she opened up about what happened on a dreadful day a couple weeks before.

"It seemed my soul knew something and it tried to warn me, but the inevitable happened before Ben even got to the doctor's appointment. He decided after years without cardio exercise that he would start running. He had been away for a business trip to the West Coast and flew back home on a Thursday. He told me while he was away, eating and sleeping poorly, he started to think about his lifestyle. He rarely worked out anymore, and he really missed the feeling of accomplishment when he finished a run. He said, 'I want to get back to running and increase my stamina — it might help me when I have to chase the kids. Besides, eating on the road hasn't been the best thing for me; too much rich food at dinners and fast food for lunch can't have a great effect on my health.' He seemed to be excited about buying new sneakers, lacing them up, and hitting the road." She wiped the corner of her eye, trying to keep back to the tears.

"I told him, 'I think is a great idea.'" She looked at me like a lost child and she continued. "I was hoping that running would help his cardio health, even though we didn't know what shape his heart was in. Monday morning he woke up early and put on the running sneakers that he purchased over the weekend. He drank a glass of water and headed out into the brisk morning in the great outdoors to challenge his forty-four-year-old body to some exercise.

"I was in the kitchen preparing breakfast and lunches for the kids when I heard him come in through the garage. I asked him, 'How did it feel?'

"He drank another glass of water and said, 'It felt good. It was nice to be outside enjoying the quiet morning and planning my day. But I can't believe how out of shape I am. I ache from head to toe. I thought I stretched well enough, but I can't get rid of this pain in my leg.'

"I reassured him, 'It's probably muscle weakness; every day you run it'll get better.' I was making the kids pancakes and offered to make extra for him.

"He kissed me on my cheek and told me he was going to hit the shower and then he'd be down.

"As I stirred the batter, I heard the shower turn on. Mathew and Annie came into the kitchen. 'Good morning, guys. Did you sleep well?'

"'Yeah, I did. I'm hungry—what's for breakfast?' I'm always amazed at how much food, especially pancakes, Mathew can pack into his flesh-and-bone body." She smiled.

"I told them I would have some pancakes ready in a couple minutes and asked Mathew to help me get out some plates."

"'What can I do, Mommy?' Annie always felt like she lived in her brother's shadow, always trying to shine brighter than him," Julie told me.

"So I looked around the kitchen, trying to find something she could easily do. I told her to get the napkins. Mathew put the plates on the island, and Annie sat in her chair, folding the napkins the best her seven-year-old fingers could. I turned back to the stove, tested the griddle with drops of water, and began to pour the pancake batter onto the sizzling hot griddle. All of a sudden this horrific thud, like something had fallen, came from upstairs. Jenny, it was horrible."

I noticed Julie's hands were shaking.

"The shower was still running. I turned off the griddle and told the kids to stay put and said I would be back. I wanted to see what could have made that sound."

She stopped talking and took a deep breath, preparing herself for what she had to tell me. "My heart was beating fast as I climbed the stairs. I thought to myself, *It was a heavy sound, not like something fell off a shelf. Like Ben fell down.* I ran into our bedroom and turned the corner into our master bath. The door was slightly open, and I could see Ben's feet on the floor." She couldn't hold back her tears any more. Julie was shaking, as if she were experiencing it for the first time. "I ran to open the door and saw his body laying still on the cold tile floor. My tall, strapping husband was lying face first on the floor, not moving at all. His back was too still for him to be taking a breath. 'Ben!' I screamed. 'Ben, wake up.' And nothing happened. I fought to turn him over, but he was so heavy. His dead weight fought against every effort I made to turn him face-up. I ran to get the cordless phone from the side of the bed, and I was able to get my frantic fingers to dial 911. I went back to Ben and called out to him. I noticed out of the corner of my eye my two sweet, darling children staring with blank looks as their father lay dying on the floor. Jenny, it was horrible. I will never forget the looks on their faces.

"As I stared blankly at the children, I heard a voice on the line. 'Nine-one-one. What's your emergency?' I remember feeling jealous of the operator's voice, even-toned and flat as glass, without emotion. How I wish I could have had the same tone. 'I need an ambulance. My husband fell and must have hit his head. I think he's dead—he's not breathing.' Then I realized the kids were still standing there watching this nightmare unfold. I turned to Mathew and instructed him to take his sister and get my cell phone and call you." Julie reached over to hold my hand.

"I was fading in and out. I realized the operator was talking to me, asking me something. 'Ma'am, please calm down. What is the address? I will send help right away.'

"I told her the address and said, 'Please come quick, I don't know what to do.'

"And then I started to cry. I understood how dire the situation that was unfolding in front of me was, and I didn't know what to do. 'Damn you, Ben, wake up. Roll over and wake up. Start laughing and tell me this is all a joke,' but that didn't happen. His body remained as I found it, lifeless. I cried.

"And I was crying when I felt an arm around me. I turned and saw your face staring at me with a concerned look."

I knew what happened next but sat silently. I knew she needed to continue, to tell the story the way she remembered it. "You took the phone from my hand and started to talk to the operator. You lifted me up; you led me to the bed to sit and wait for help. Alex must have been right behind you, because I remember hearing his voice yell at Ben to wake up, followed by the force of his breath into Ben's mouth and then a thumping sound when he tried to pump life back into his good friend's body. We both sat there and listened to that rhythm for what seemed like a lifetime, waiting for the rescue team to come running and bring Ben back to life."

I looked at Julie, my tears dropping to the table. There was no use in trying to stop them; nothing could stop the flow as I listened to the details as my best friend retold the horrible story of the day she lost her husband.

"I have a hint of a memory of you telling me, 'Julie, Nicolas and Jessica are with the kids in the playroom. The ambulance is almost here. Everything will be okay.' I looked at you, thinking, *She is so wrong. Nothing will ever be okay again. My husband is dead.* A lonely tear fell from my eye. It must have been left behind in hope that the outcome would be different.

"You left me to open the door for the EMTs. After several minutes of unsuccessful attempts to revive Ben, they had the shell of my husband's life loaded on a stretcher. They carried him though the front door, the same door that greeted our guests and friends when they would come to visit. That would be his final pass through it."

We sat silently for a while. I could hear the commotion and healthy laughter of the kids in the playroom. I was hoping Julie felt it was cathartic to share with me her memories of what happened to Ben, knowing I wouldn't judge. I reached out to hold her hand. "Julie, nothing could have prevented it. The doctors told us it was unavoidable, given his family history." I tried to think of something more to say to ease my friend's suffering. But I realized that, as with my aunt Sally's death, no one could say anything to take away the pain and loss after losing a loved one. I could only sit and be there for her.

The week before Julie shared her story with me, we were planning the funeral of her husband. The rain fell hard as light broke the darkness that had surrounded our homes while we slept. What I wouldn't have given to roll over and fall back to sleep, to not face the day ahead of me. As I shook Alex to wake him from his peaceful slumber, I knew we had to get up. Julie needed us.

"Is it time to wake up already? I was having a dream, a great dream. I was playing hockey, and I was on a breakaway, just me and the goalie. Just as I was able to shoot the puck, I got checked." Shaking his head and messing up his bed head, he said, "Just as I got checked, I felt you shaking me. It was strange—you were the player checking me." Wrapping his arms around me, he said, "Isn't it weird how real life can play out in your dreams?"

Being in his arms was the safest place in the world. "Yes, it is." He had no idea how well I could identify with that.

The tent at the graveside memorial, set up under a tree, protected us from the falling rain. I was lost in the pitter-patter of raindrops hitting the canopy. As I stared at the ground, I noticed the tiny discolored brown, red, and yellow leaves that had fallen to the ground, suffering the same fate as Ben. They once lived high above, sheltering us from the heat of the sun and creating shadows on the ground below, and now they lay, fallen. They had completed their journey and would be replaced next year by new leaves that would become our protectors. My thoughts drifted to Julie. *Who will protect her now that Ben is gone?*

Julie, the woman I called my best friend, who used to light up a room when she walked in, now looked as though she had only a fraction of that light remaining. Too weak to hold her umbrella, her hands shook. She held onto a handkerchief that looked like one of Ben's. Her shoulders slumped forward and down. She was so lost in her emotions she didn't seem to notice her children walk up behind her with her parents. Annie tugged onto Julie's skirt hem, seeming to break the rollercoaster of thoughts bombarding Julie's mind.

Looking down at Annie and then Mathew, Julie cried, making no sound. I stepped closer to Alex, thankful he was there with me, thinking how easily I could be in Julie's place right now—'but for the grace of God there go I.' I thought, *Why her?*

My life had been so blessed—every dream and wish I made had come true—but I found myself beginning to worry that someday it would all fall apart. I could be standing at my husband's graveside, shedding tears over what was and scared to think of what would be.

Alex reached for my hand as if he knew what I was thinking; his warm touch reminded me of the life I still had. I looked up to meet his gaze, and his hand wrapped tighter around mine. *I need to stop torturing myself with worry. My life is good.*

A few nights later, I woke up after having a dream that was really more of a nightmare. The haunting spell it placed in me left me with a feeling I couldn't shake. The nightmare images played out in my mind's eye, dark images of masked people moving away from me; it appeared they had Alex with them. They were encircled him, guiding him. I called out to him. "Alex, where are you going?" There was no answer. He didn't even turn his head. As he walked away, surrounded by the dark images, I began to see shadows of tree limbs shaped like fingers, motioning for Alex to follow. Black cats ran beside the masked crowd; black crows were crying out for him and swooping overhead. I felt the movement of air across my face created by the flapping wings. I stopped to look around and saw that I was standing on piles of human bones, and shivers went down my back.

Then I heard dark eerie voices speaking in unison: "He's coming with us, he's with us. He's coming with us, he's with us."

"No! You can't take him!" I yelled. I needed to get to Alex and free him.

They kept moving away from me. I struggled to run, to keep up, but my legs wouldn't move. It seemed the harder I tried to run, the more deeply I was swallowed into the remains of those people who had come this way before. I was sinking into the pit of bones. I needed to get out to reach Alex. I called out to him again, "Alex! Alex, come back."

I shot up in bed breathing heavily. *It was just a dream*, I told myself over and over, trying to convince myself Alex was okay. I looked over and saw him lying in bed, sleeping like an angel, unaware of the horrifying dream that stole another of my peaceful night's sleep.

The images that plagued me during my nightmares had me convinced Alex was going to die. All the images that controlled my dream—the darkness, the black cats, the black crows, the skeleton bones and the faceless, black-caped auras—were signs of death. There was no mistaking it. As I took deep breaths and laid back down, I tried to tell myself it was crazy to think that—it was just a dream. I knew I had become fragile after being witness as Julie mourned the death of Ben; his passing had triggered me to relive the loss of my aunt. My subconscious was overloaded with the "what if" scenarios that had been stirring up my worries during the daytime hours. But what if it was a premonition? In the middle of the night, surrounded by darkness, exhausted, I worried what life would be like without Alex. I shuddered at the thought and rolled over to wrap my arms around the anchor in my life. I pulled in close to his back. Feeling more secure, I waited for sleep to take me away, praying for a sweeter dream this time.

A week passed by after my nightmare about Alex dying. I appreciated the peaceful dreams that had entertained some of my nights, but I was challenged to find a full night's sleep due to my hormones. At my recent physical, I told my doctor I was suffering from night sweats, had trouble sleeping, and was experiencing anxiety. I explained about the sense of doom and my fears of losing Alex. Based on those symptoms at the age of forty-two, in her opinion my body was entering the unpredictable stage in life of perimenopause. While most days I still felt young and vibrant, the doctor's blanket statement about my body's changes left me feeling old and dried up.

I got out of bed to start another day, and after a busy morning rushing to get the kids off to school, I told them, "See you after school." I kissed both kids before they got on the bus.

I am always amazed at how fast two hours can pass by and how little I seem to get done. *I'm so busy helping the kids get ready for their day and getting myself ready, it leaves no time breathe.* Some friends wake up at the crack of dawn and exercise and shower before their kids place one foot in the kitchen. I have tried to start a workout routine before the kids wake up, only to have it interrupted because of my nighttime visitors. Either Nicolas or Jessica disturbs my sleep on any given night. It's as if the kids know I'm making a change in my life and they're out to sabotage it.

The last time I tried to get up early didn't work very well because Jessica was in my room every hour that night with nightmares. Every time I told her she was safe and walked her back to her room and told her to get back to sleep, within the hour I heard the little padded socked feet running down the hall to my room again. In the morning I forced myself out of bed and proceeded with a half-assed workout. I talked myself out of a shower because I hadn't sweated too much and I was so tired. Instead, I put on some deodorant, pulled my hair into a smoother ponytail, and I confess I stayed in my workout clothes all day. Now I tell myself, or fool myself, that it's better to sleep until the kids wake me. After they leave for school, I promise to go to the treadmill and get my exercise when I am full of energy and ready to put in the extra effort.

Today, I woke up tired before I even put my feet on the floor because of hormone-induced insomnia. I needed one more jolt from a cup of coffee after I spent a good part of the night tossing and turning. I guess it comes with age; the good old hormones are wreaking havoc on more than my moods. Before I got on the treadmill, I poured the decadent black energy booster into the hand-painted pink and purple mug the kids had made at the pottery place for Mother's Day. I decided to turn on the television for entertainment while I drank the extra cup of coffee; it seemed like a good idea at the time.

I held onto the warm, colorful mug like it was a security blanket, and I watched and listened to the television hosts announce their next segment on relationship issues.

"We have an interesting concept coming up next. How differently would you treat someone if you knew they only had one year left to live?" They had my attention. I sat up and listened.

"Well, Ryan, that sounds like an interesting discussion. Maybe I should pay attention. I could stand to treat my mother-in-law a little better." Laughter broke out on the set, and they cut to a commercial. After a quick trip to the bathroom, I was back in front of the television; like a schoolgirl watching her favorite show, I didn't want to miss a second of it.

The idea seemed relatively interesting. If a person had issues with another person and found out the other person only had one year to live, certainly they would be more sympathetic toward the person. It would almost be like having a teacher you didn't get along with. You could survive it, knowing you would only be together for one year and then you would move on. I started to think about the people in life you loved and cared about. How sad would it be to know that they had only one year left to live, like people who are diagnosed with diseases and told they only have months or years to live?

As the hosts chatted back and forth with their psychologist guest, I thought about my life. How would I feel if I knew I only had one year left to live? Just as my hormones ran wild in my body, my thoughts started running wild as well. I started thinking about the nightmares I had. What if Alex only had one year to live? As I sat in the chair staring at the television, my body became numb. I didn't hear a thing the talk show hosts were saying as my irrational thoughts took over my ability to think clearly. If Alex were to die, had I done enough to show him how much I loved and cared about him? I recognized I was about to lose it, so I tried to calm myself down; I took a breath. But my emotions were all over the place because of the damn hormones raging in my bloodstream. I thought about losing Alex like Julie had lost Ben and my grandparents and mother had lost my aunt Sally. I noticed tears were running down my cheeks, dropping like raindrops into what was supposed to be a cup full of energy-enhancing liquid. But it had become a cup full of dread. Walking to the sink, I poured the coffee down the drain and told myself I should have just gotten on the treadmill.

Later that day my mother and I sat at her kitchen table, the teapot screaming, "I'm hot, I'm ready." It was a rare afternoon when I had nothing to do, so I went by my parent's house for a visit.

"Just honey, right?" my mother asked as she poured hot water into the mug that held a chamomile teabag.

"Yeah, that's all I need. Thanks, Mom." I got up from my seat and gazed out the window into the back yard, remembering the night Alex proposed to me. It was one of the happiest moments of my life.

I sat opposite my mother, stirring my tea and blending the flavors together. I brought up the nightmares I had been experiencing and the television show I'd watched earlier.

"Mom, I need to talk to you about something. I'm worried about losing Alex." The words were barely out of my mouth before my mother pinched her lips together to keep from spitting tea.

"What are you talking about, Jenny? Is there something going on your father and I don't know about?" Her face showed her concern.

"No, not in that way. It's just I keep having nightmares, and this morning I watched a talk show about death. Let's not forget that I'm also watching helplessly as Julie tries to move through life without her husband. It's all weighing on me, I think."

"The mind is powerful, Jenny." She took a sip of her tea, "Look at what you know. Nightmares are, simply put, thoughts you didn't reconcile during the day. Alex is healthy, right?"

I nod in confirmation.

"All right then. What is there to worry about?"

"We thought Ben was healthy, and look what happened to him. Also, another haunting thought I keep having is that Alex is almost the same age as Aunt Sally was when she died, and that came as such a shock to my life."

My mother shook her head, and a sad expression spilled across her face. She remembered all too well the shock of losing her only sister.

"I just don't know what I would do if I lost him. Mom, he is everything to me." The tea bag playfully tickled the water as I moved it up and down in the mug, and I stared at the waves it left behind before continuing. "I started wondering—if he died, would he know how much I loved him? We have been so busy raising kids, I don't think we've taken the time to tell each other how important we are to one another.

"I enjoy the time I spend volunteering in the kids' classes. It fulfills the part of me that loves to teach. The part I gave up to stay at home to raise the kids. On the days I finish volunteering at school, I welcome the kids home from school, and when Alex's workday is done, we taxi Nicolas and Jessica to sports practice or their other activities. Now he's in fifth grade, Nicolas is playing travel soccer this spring, and Jessica is taking ballet lessons and playing soccer. It's no wonder we collapse at the end of the day, Alex on the couch and me in my chair. Some nights we don't even sit in the same room to watch television. Our lives have taken on a new dynamic—everything we do is for the kids. I don't think it's working very well for us." I breathed in fresh air, hoping it would cleanse my mind after my rant.

I felt the warmth of her hand and saw the love in my mother's eyes. She said, "Then take the time, Jenny. Show him and tell him how much he means to you. No one knows the exact time a person will die. It's very important to be aware of how we treat the ones we love and to make sure they know they are loved. Even though I lost your Aunt Sally too soon, we knew we loved each other. I don't think differently about it. She left this world with as much love as she could take with her."

I smiled, "You're right, Mom. I guess I need to make sure I give Alex as much love and attention as I can and appreciate the time we have together, because in the end, love is all there really is." I smiled, realizing those were the words my mother had said to me my whole life.

My mom hugged me close. I felt warm, reassured that I would appreciate my future days with Alex. I thanked her for listening and told her I loved her, the same words she always spoke to me. After I helped clean up from our afternoon tea, I left to get home before the kids got off the bus. As I drove down the winding roads that led me to the place where I felt the most comfortable, I promised myself I was not going to waste a minute with Alex. I would shower him with the most affection I had ever given him and would make sure I gave our relationship more attention. I took a personal oath during my drive home on that sunny spring day to spread joy in my husband's life, hoping it would fill both of us with an endless amount of love, so that in the end neither of us would ever forget the depth of our love for each other.

Alex

"NO, NO!"

I feel the covers sliding over my body like a wave washing over a stone. I hear a soft voice crying out, and I realize Jenny is dreaming. I don't know what she's dreaming about, but whatever is happening, she is being tormented.

"Jenny, wake up. You're dreaming."

She continues to repeat herself. "No, no."

I shake her, not too hard but hard enough to wake her. "Wake up, Jenny." When I touch her, she is soaking wet. It must be a really bad dream. She takes a deep breath, and then she turns to me with tears in her eyes.

"Oh my, Alex. That was the worst one I have ever had." Her arms wrap around me, and she buries her face into my chest.

"Do you want to tell me about it?" I rub her back, wishing could do more to comfort her.

"I was in a dark room, I think it was raining. You know how when you dream, your mind fills in things you can't see? It was like that. The room was decorated like an office, and as I walked into it I noticed the bookcases at the far end reached from the floor to ceiling, and every shelf held a book or a decoration. There was a mahogany desk in the right corner. A small desk lamp barely glowed. There were two chairs opposite the desk. I walked to the desk, my feet feeling heavy. Every step felt like I was walking in thick mud. I wanted to go forward, but my feet didn't want to bring me there.

"I noticed when I got to the desk that the lamp spread its dim light over the surface of the desk, highlighting a calendar. October was written in big letters across the top; every day was numbered and they were blank, except for October twenty-second." I noticed her breathing become heavier, but I urged her to continue.

"This is the part that scared me and freaked me out, because I don't understand it. As I focused in on the date, I noticed it was circled in the shape of a heart with a red marker. The freaky thing is as I stared longer at it, it changed from a red marker to red blood, and then the blood began creeping down the calendar page." She sat up on her elbows. "What do you think it means?"

"Jenny, I know it was scary and freaked you out, but it's hard know what dreams mean. I'm sure it was nothing. Did you cut yourself today and bleed?"

"No." She sounded a million miles away. I could tell she was wracking her brain, trying to find some meaning in the nightmare.

"Sleep close to me, I'll keep you safe." I kissed the top of her head and pulled her into my chest. I would always protect her and keep her safe.

The next morning Jenny seemed distant and bothered when I tried to help her get the kids ready for school. She cooked breakfast in slow motion, like she was a drone.

"Jenny, sit down. Let me help you." I walked her over to the island stool and placed her coffee in front of her. I dropped down onto my elbows, and, looking into her eyes, I told her, "Jenny, I know the dream really got to you, but it's just that, a dream. Think of all the dreams or nightmares you've had. Have any of them ever come true?" She remained speechless. "See? This one is just another trick your mind is playing on you. Don't let it ruin your day, please." I kissed her cheek and began eating breakfast. Jenny sat, staring at the steam rising from her mug. I looked back at her as she sat there and told myself she would be okay.

I couldn't figure out when the change happened, but at some point I sensed a new feeling coming from Jenny. Things were different as we moved through our days. She called more often to talk during the day, and in general she was more available to me.

Jenny was still having a hard time sleeping. We didn't talk about it, but I knew she was restless most nights. After the nightmare about the calendar and the blood, she never told me about any other nightmares she had. She did mention that at her last physical her doctor had told her she was likely going through hormonal changes. Some women her age she knew were going through changes too and having more difficulty sleeping, but with Jenny it was a bit different. Her nightmares were a sign she was facing a deeper struggle. I wanted to help her, so I did research on perimenopause. The information I gathered helped to explain a lot of the changes Jenny was experiencing, but she refused to talk to me about her feelings and her emotions. She said I wouldn't understand because I was a guy. I assured her I was always available to listen. I knew that when she was ready to share her feelings, she would. I wasn't going to push her.

In the meantime I enjoyed the attention she was giving me. Our relationship and our lives had changed as the kids grew older. Nicolas would be eleven in a couple months and Jessica would turn eight soon after. They were becoming more demanding of our time, and by the end of the day I had all I could do to keep from falling asleep on the couch. Jenny and I had our special ways of showing each other we were still in love at night, even though our days keep us busy and apart. And I often left her love notes in random places, like her car visor or in between the towels in our bathroom. The more random the place, the better her reaction. I looked forward to the phone call that let me know she found one. I loved her with all my heart, and I wanted her to always know she was in my thoughts, even though it seemed like I was moving a hundred miles in the other direction. Although I might have been distracted by work and the kids, she was always on my mind.

When Jenny started to treat me differently, my memories flashed back to the early years of our marriage. Like most couples starting out in a new marriage, Jenny and I spent most of our time together, and we hosted parties with friends. Everything was new, and I shared every experience with my new life partner. Life felt fresh. But now, with Jenny showering me with affection and offering me free time to spend with friends, I was unsure how to accept what was happening.

I first noticed the changes on a Sunday. Jenny got out of bed and told me, "Stay in bed and doze. No need to come downstairs early. I'll feed the kids, and you can have the morning to yourself. I'll bring your coffee and the newspaper up in a bit." She kissed my cheek and headed to the bathroom.

At first I was shocked. The offer was uncharacteristic of her, because she was the one who enjoyed a Sunday morning coffee in bed. I hadn't indulged in it in a long time, since we were first married. Back then we would share a couple cups of coffee while reading the newspaper in bed, and it always led to a happy Sunday morning delight. Those good times lasted about a year before we started taking our coffees to the family room, but I admit, I missed those days.

Then as the sleepy fog lifted from my brain and I became more awake, I thought, *Thanks honey, this is great!* I could read the paper and enjoy my coffee without distractions; no little monkeys climbing on me and begging for my attention.

I thought it was sure to be a onetime deal, but as the months passed, Jenny brought me coffee every Sunday. I told her she was spoiling me and I didn't need to continue this every Sunday, but she insisted, telling me it was good for me to have alone time. I wasn't about to argue with that.

We spent our Saturday mornings watching the kids play soccer. It was family time, and neither of us missed a game. Jenny and I enjoyed watching Nicolas and Jessica race up and down the field chasing after the white and black round ball. They played on separate teams, which meant a full morning of soccer. When work scheduled a golf outing on the day of the last soccer game, I knew that would be the first time I wasn't at the field to see the kids play. I thought Jenny would be very disappointed, but, much to my surprise, she encouraged me to play golf and stay for the following awards ceremony and dinner.

"Alex, I think it's a great idea. This weekend it supposed to be beautiful—sunny, with temperatures in the seventies, perfect weather for the golf course." She was smiling, and I was confused. I wasn't expecting that reaction. She said, "I'll explain it to the kids. They'll understand."

I walked up to Jenny and I touched her forehead to see if she had a fever. "Are you feeling okay? I thought you would be upset and not want me to go."

She held my arms in her hands and said, "Alex, you work very hard to provide for our family. I don't think it's unreasonable for you to enjoy a Saturday out on the golf course." She turned to put a dish in the dishwasher. "And while you are at it, I think you should schedule a tee time for every Saturday morning. Maybe you could see if you're friend Stephen wants to join you. I'm sure Melissa would let him sneak away for the morning."

I stood in our kitchen, shocked. I wasn't sure I'd heard Jenny right. *Did she tell me to schedule a tee time every Saturday?*

"Did I hear you right? Jenny, you know that means I'll miss family day. I don't know if I could do that to the kids."

"Well, if every Saturday is too much, then play every other. I just want you to be happy and know you have my blessing to play. I know how much you enjoy it." She stood with her back against the cabinet, a loving smile on her face.

"Jenny, you are the best the wife in the world. No other wife I know would insist their husband play golf on the weekends. Most of them nag and tell them not to." I gave her a big bear hug, feeling like the luckiest man in the world to have a wife so understanding and loving.

As I received more of Jenny's blessings with every request I made. It became obvious that she was up to something. I waited for the day when she would lay out her laundry list of demands for weekends away with girlfriends to make up for all the free time she had given to me, as if they had been deposits into a bank account labeled Your Free Time = My Free Time. Yet every time I tried to ask her what she was up to, she would look at me like I was an alien and tell me, "It's all for love."

"Jenny, I know you're playing me. Why have you been granting me all this freedom?" We sat in the family room after the kids were in bed for the night; my feet rested on the ottoman.

"Alex, I love you. Is there anything wrong with that or allowing you to spend some time alone and with friends?" She sat across from me curled up in her girly chair with flowers swirling on it.

"It just seems like you turned on a light switch and are now giving me more affection and pushing me away on the weekends. I'm confused. Don't get me wrong, I appreciate it, but I don't understand why you're doing it."

"The only reason why I'm doing it is because I love you." She moved over to the couch and straddled my lap. She kissed me with tender lips and then pulled back and stared into my eyes. "I want you to know that I love you."

And when she started to show me how she loved me with her lips on mine, I stopped questioning her motives. Being a man, it really was that easy.

Jenny

IT HAD BEEN MONTHS SINCE I BEGAN CATERING TO ALEX, SHOWING my affection and attention for him, and he was very confused about my intentions. I reassured him that everything I did was from a loving place in my heart. Giving him Saturdays to golf and Sunday mornings in bed gave me more time with the kids, and since they were in school all day, I had found myself missing their presence. I had become comfortable with them being home as toddlers and felt a bit disconnected from them as they became school-age kids. I didn't mind the extra time with them, and I felt good knowing I was fulfilling my oath to myself to bring joy and love to Alex's life.

My favorite way of showing my love toward Alex was through cooking his favorite meals. He loved to eat rich, hearty dinners, but when our lives became more focused on the kids' lives and schedules, I had found myself cooking fast meals, with little effort or love put into them. Under my new regimen, I organized my shopping list around the meals I knew Alex loved the most. It was probably the favorite change I had made since the nightmares that hinted he was going to die, taking my life support system with him.

As the school year began to come to an end, I realized we had no vacation plans for the summer. During my morning run, as I listened to the pat-pat-pat of my feet hitting the ground and the rhythmic movement of air in and out of my lungs, I thought hard about the places Alex had wanted to visit but for various reasons we never got to go. Then I came up with our destination, the best trip for us to go on. I ran around the corner to the top of our street and felt light as air with delight. As I approached our house I noticed Alex's car in the driveway. Perfect—he came home for something and now I could tell him about our summer vacation plans.

"Alex? Where are you?" I burst through the door. I found him in his office looking through a stack of papers. Still out of breath I said, "Guess where we are going this summer?"

"Uh, I don't know." He didn't seem a bit interested, but instead rather annoyed by my interruption.

"Alaska!" I could hardly contain my enthusiasm.

"Alaska? Why?" The look on his face matched the confusion in his voice, but I had his attention.

"You silly! I know you have always wanted to go there. I won the debate over our honeymoon to Bermuda, and we have put off going to Alaska for more convenient trips. The kids will be finishing school soon, and it will be a good time to go. Besides, it's a great educational trip for the kids too. We can go for hikes in the national parks or go kayaking. Jessica will love looking for sea lions, otters, and other wildlife. It'll be our summer vacation." Happiness poured out of me through my words.

"I don't know about this, Jenny. How much will a trip like this cost?" His stress wrinkle, right between his eyes in his third-eye spot, became deeper by the second.

"I'll look into it, but please don't worry about the money, Alex. Family vacations are priceless! I was thinking we could leave in the beginning of July, after Nicolas's birthday."

Alex's confusion was replaced with happiness. He knew there was no sense in arguing with me; he always gave in. "Well, it seems you've got it all planned, and I'm going to Alaska!" As we hugged, I knew I was going to give my husband the best gift ever, a trip of a lifetime. I was thrilled to see his excitement when it registered that he was going on his dream vacation to Alaska.

As the vacation date approached, our excitement grew, and the anticipation was hard to control. The kids were thrilled to be going away for two weeks and taking an airplane ride to explore the sights of Alaska. Nicolas studied every book the library had on Alaska. He familiarized himself with all the attractions in the areas where we were going, but he was most excited about the cruise we were taking in Glacier Bay. Jessica looked in books to find out what animals she would see — any would do. She would have her camera and be ready to snap a picture to showcase her discoveries.

The trip was everything we thought it would be. From the ship we saw whales, seals, and sea lions. One morning during our walk around the deck, we noticed a group of people gathered at one section of the ship. Nicolas and Jessica ran ahead of us to see what the group was staring at. When they saw the orca whale, they started yelling for us to come. We watched as the large black and white creature swam like a ballerina, so graceful, through the waves the ship left behind. It swam next to us and jumped out of the water, showing off its moves, and then splashed back down. As we watched the beautiful display, I looked at the kids' faces. I knew it would be their favorite memory.

We ended our trip with a camping excursion in Bartlett Cove. It was the first time the kids had experienced living outdoors. We kayaked around Bartlett Cove and made daytrips to the Beardslee Islands. Sitting in a kayak and looking at the land rise out of the ocean to become tall peaks made me realize how small I was. We were surrounded by water, with glaciers all around us. It was truly inspiring to see the formations reflecting colors as the sun shone brightly; the blue sky reflected off the glaciers, bathing them in a blue hue that bounced off the white formations, creating textures that played off the light of the sun. The shadows of the dark crevices on the glaciers and the sun's rays penetrating down produced brilliant streaks of multiple blue tones through the surfaces of the glaciers.

We enjoyed daily hikes on the beach and in the forested area, always keeping our eyes open in search of wild animals. Jessica, our animal lover, was thrilled when she saw a porcupine scurry up a tree. Alex and Nicolas tried fly fishing for the first time and were looking like professionals by the end of trip, although their catches didn't always prove it. But they caught a big one on their last day; a perfect way to end our trip.

As we began the long plane ride home, the kids shared their thoughts about how much they'd enjoyed the trip.

"My favorite part was fishing with Daddy." Nicolas was looking at the picture of the last fish he and Alex caught. The trout was marked with black spots that were uniformly placed along its body; the top half of the body was olive green, and a pink line separated its top half from the bottom half. As I looked over Nicolas's shoulder at the picture, I noticed that two of the fish fins were the same color pink as the stripe; the other fins were a lighter shade of green with black spots. It was a remarkable-looking fish. I'd never seen a fish with more vibrant colors. The best part was knowing that Alex and Nicolas caught him together. I knew Nicolas would never forget that day.

Jessica loved watching the black bear we'd spotted when we were hiking in the woods. "Mommy, I loved seeing the bear the most. He looked so cuddly. I really wanted to run up to him and hug him, but I know you wouldn't have let me." She hugged the stuffed bear in her arms. "But I also loved the whale swimming with our ship — that was cool."

While the kids were engrossed in their mementos, Alex and I talked about how special the trip was to him. He held my hand in his as he spoke.

"Jenny, I don't think I could ever tell you how much this trip has meant to me. For years I have wanted to see and experience what Alaska was like. It was better than I ever imagined." He put his head back on the seat and closed his eyes for a moment. Then, looking back at me, he continued. "Being able to see it with you and give the kids the opportunity to experience it is something I will never forget. Thank you so much. I love you."

"Alex, I'm glad I could plan it and organize it for you." Holding his hand and tracing his knuckles with my finger, I told him, "You know I'm a dreamer, and I believe that everyone should be able to live their dreams, but I also know it can be hard for people to find the time to plan something they may think is excessive."

Alex nudged my shoulder with his.

"Well, I really appreciate it, Jenny. Thank you." He kissed my lips softly.

When we landed at the airport, the kids were curled up in their seats, asleep, and I hated to wake them. It had been an exhausting vacation, but one we would all remember forever, and that's just the way I wanted it.

Jenny

AS THE SUMMER PASSED AND WE MOVED INTO THE FALL MONTHS, I was filled with love. It turns out that giving Alex more attention and time to himself had caused a stir in him, and he began to show me more love. My thoughts and fears about losing Alex didn't change, however. In fact, the more I gave myself to him, the deeper our love grew and the deeper the dread of losing him became.

On nights when I can't sleep, I sit here in the quiet hush of our gourmet kitchen and think, usually about my fear of Alex not being with me to share my life. The light from the stove casts shadows around my kitchen. I stir my tea, creating small waves in the mug. The green numbers on the microwave inform me that I'm right on time for my date with insomnia. I can't shake the haunting feeling that follows me through my days, like shadows cast by the sun, that the charmed relationship I have with Alex could be ending soon. I am awake most nights. My despair and the dreadful possibility that he could be taken from me fill me with deep insecurities. I shudder. How will I continue without the one person who has been there all along?

Alex is my true best friend, the one I can rely on to help me with all life's troubles, and at the age of forty-two, I still feel overjoyed at the sight of him. When all my girlfriends left me for their careers or boyfriends, he was there for me. He was always the first one I called with news, good or bad. He is my rock, my strength, my love — my life. Like all couples, we have been through our share of rough patches, but in the end every challenge has always strengthened our love and determination to continue to grow with each other. As we've experienced our lives together, we have learned how to use the darker days of life and life's trials grow closer.

All the things Alex and I haven't experienced together yet, like watching our children grow to become adults and sharing the experience of being grandparents, would be unfulfilled dreams without him. The thought of growing old without him there to hold my hand when life gets scary and not having him by my side when I need him the most disturbs me, making me realize once more how precious our time together is. I am afraid. I fear losing another person who has always been there for me.

I try to replace my negative thoughts. I always begin with the time when I first saw Alex. I relive our first years; feelings of warm love radiate through my soul. A deeper knowing of how special our love is fills me, and I am content.

I still didn't want to miss an opportunity to show him how much love I had for him. On some level I knew the extra effort I put into everything to show him my love was crazy. I had a daily contest with myself to see which part of me, the crazy side or the rational being within me, would win the struggle to tell myself that my dreams, or rather my nightmares, meant nothing. I was merely living a life full of fear because of my neighbor's sudden death and losing my aunt at such a young age so many years ago.

The suddenness of both deaths, especially my aunt Sally's, had created a deep wound in my life. Every time it would start to heal and scab over, I would see someone who looked like my aunt Sally, or I'd think I heard her voice in a crowd, or I'd experience something that reminded me of her. The scab would rip off, and the heavy feeling of loss I suffered after she died returned. Sipping my tea, I relived the early days without her.

Filled with grief, I had stood next to my aunt's casket, my hands folded in an attempt to stop them from shaking. I had a hard time understanding how we could be mourning the loss of her life. Less than a week before she was alive and seemed healthy. Then she died of a sudden heart attack. Aunt Sally was like a second mother to me, or maybe more like the older sister I never had. Growing up my aunt Sally was my role model.

People often mistook us for mother and daughter when I was little, and when I got older they thought we were sisters. I looked more like my aunt than I did my mother. Sally and I both had brown hair and brown eyes, although her eyes were a deeper shade of dark chocolate. Her skin was clear and radiant; she had a natural beauty.

Sally never got married or had children of her own, so I was like the daughter she never had. When I was growing up, Aunt Sally took me shopping to the cool stores to buy clothes. When I got my driver's permit, she was the only person comfortable enough to let me drive. We would go for long drives to the beach and get ice cream. We sat at the beach and had conversations about growing up and any difficult decisions I had to make.

Sally knew about all my boyfriends and the teenage heartaches I suffered; she knew all of my deepest and darkest secrets. We talked about sex the summer before my high school junior year. I had not had a sexual experience, but most of my friends had. I was confused and didn't know who to talk to about it. When we were at the beach and I had told Aunt Sally I was going to have sex with a football player because I just wanted to know how it felt. My friends were always talking about their experiences while I just sat there silently, feeling awkward that I had nothing to add.

Jim, a senior on the football team, asked me out, and I was quite excited an older boy wanted to date me. We were planning on going to the movies and then meeting up with friends at a kid's house whose parents were out of town. It would be the perfect time to do it. I knew the outfit I would wear and the perfect bra and undies. I would make the experience as perfect as I could, so I would feel satisfied and be able to talk to my friends about how great sex was.

As I told Aunt Sally about my plans, she started shaking her head. I couldn't understand why she was upset. Everyone I knew was either having sex or had already done it. Sally explained to me that the first time should be special, an experience shared with someone I cared about and who cared about me. Having sex wasn't something I should just do to say I had done it or to fit in.

Then she shared the first time she had a serious a relationship with a boy; his name was John. They went to the same high school and met in science class. After they had been dating for four months they had sex. She described the experience with a tear in her eye and sadness in her voice. She held my hand while she talked.

"He wasn't an athlete, but he had a nice body. He was tall, with blond hair and blue eyes. He was really smart, and he enjoyed helping me study for my classes. He cared so much for me that he didn't want to do anything I wasn't ready for." She turned to face me. "That's the difference, Jenny. You want the boy to really care about you. Sex is a big step and comes with a lot of responsibility. Anyway, about seven months after our relationship got serious, he found out he was moving."

I watched the sadness unfold in her eyes.

"My heart was broken. I'd given myself to him in a way that I had never done before, and then, like that—" she snapped her fingers— "he was gone. And with him went my heart. I never heard from him or saw him again."

"Oh, Aunt Sally, that is so sad. I never knew that happened to you." She had me thinking about my plans. Maybe I wasn't ready. I didn't want to be known as an easy girl, and I wanted the fairy tale—and the romance.

Standing with my hand on her casket, I thought about that conversation with her. I appreciated her sharing her story, which influenced me to not rush into having sex with Jim. I'm glad I waited to be in a loving relationship and could experience what true love was before having sex. In the end I did get my fairy tale. I looked over to see Alex waiting for me by the door of the funeral home, smiling at me.

I stared at Alex. I was happy he was my first and only sexual partner. I remembered the first time we had sex, during a long weekend when his parents went away. The experience was everything my aunt told me it should be. I remember being aroused even before I felt his tender touch on my skin. Just the thought of being in his bed, closer to him than I had ever been before, excited me. I laid in his bed, on his blue sheets, the scent of his cologne surrounding me, and he was patient as he touched and pleasured me. As I became one with him, I felt like I was drifting in paradise. At that moment I knew I had saved myself for the right person.

I had fumbled around his body, not sure where or how to touch him or how to please him. He showed me how he liked it and gave me time to practice to make him feel satisfied. He taught me things about my body that I never knew, and he touched me and made my skin tingle until I thought I would explode in ecstasy. For three days, we played with each other's bodies like we were exploring new land. By the end of the weekend, I became a woman as we moved in unison in, on, and around the bed.

I walked around the funeral home, looking at the pictures of Aunt Sally we'd chosen, from her childhood to the most recent one from my mother's birthday the week before her death. Losing my aunt changed my world and the lives of all the people how knew her. We would never be the same without her here. My aunt Sally had been the one person I could confide in about my relationship with Alex and my other insecurities about life. Now who would I turn to? Knowing she wouldn't be there to talk to left an empty space and an ache in my heart.

Tears ran down my cheeks, leaving streaks in my makeup. I kept asking myself how someone could die so young. She was only forty-three, with many years ahead of her and so many experiences waiting. Looking at my family and seeing the pain in their eyes was unbearable to me. My grandparents were aching to have their daughter back. As I watched them grieve, I wondered if they wished it had been one of them. I watched my mother as she talked to people offering their condolences; from the outside she looked poised, but I knew she was a mess over losing her only sister. They had been best friends since childhood. It hurt very much to watch the people I loved and admired fall apart.

Jenny

AFTER ALL THE TIME I SPENT EITHER PRAYING OR TALKING TO MY mother, I still couldn't shake the haunting feeling from the night terrors that Alex would be taken from me. Night was the hardest time for me; instead of worrying about the nightmares, I tried to persuade myself to think of other things as I laid in bed at night. When a dark thought about losing Alex crept into my mind, I thought instead of new ways to shower him with my love and reminded myself to be aware and appreciate him more than I thought I ever could.

If my irrational side was right, and it was to happen that I would lose Alex, I was determined to make every living second count. If my rational side won the contest and assured me I wasn't going to lose him, I knew I would at least have fun coming up with ideas to show my love for him. In all of the new ways I was showing my love for Alex, he loved my cooking the best, and cooking during the fall season was so much easier than in the summer. The days were getting cooler, and with the kids in school, I could more readily plan and cook meals. The season encouraged hearty homemade meals of meat, potatoes, vegetables, and gravies rich in flavor. Those were Alex's favorite dinners, and I added my love into every dish.

On a beautiful sunny fall afternoon, Alex had finished raking leaves and was just sitting down to watch the doubleheader baseball game between the Red Sox and the Orioles. I had been to the store earlier that Sunday with the kids, but they were grumpy about being there too long, so I had rushed to finish. Now I wished I had taken my time.

"Alex, I need to run to the grocery store. I forgot to get mushrooms for the chicken marsala," I yelled into the family room as I grabbed my car keys. "Who wants to come with me?" I sarcastically asked Nicolas and Jessica.

"Not me."

"Not me." They ran out of the room.

Boston was wrapping up their season, and Alex had mentioned that morning he wanted to sit and relax in front of the game. He was settling in to watch the game, but he offered to go to the store for me. "Jenny, I'll go get the mushrooms. You've already been to the store once," he called.

"No, it's okay, Alex. I don't want you to miss the baseball game." I stepped into the room, where he sat in front of the TV. "You deserve to watch it. I know you've been excited for it all day. I should be back in about thirty minutes. Everything is prepped and ready. Watch the game *and the kids*," I said with a quirky smile and gave Alex a little peck on his lips.

Alex

I WAS COMPLETELY ENGROSSED IN THE GAME. BOSTON WAS KILLING the Orioles, and I hadn't noticed how much time had passed. When I looked at the clock and saw it had been an hour since Jenny left, I reached for my cell phone to call her. I got no answer. It wasn't like her not to answer, unless she was getting her hair done. Maybe she was in an area with bad reception. *I'll give it a few minutes and try again*, I thought to myself.

My second, third, and fourth attempts went unanswered as well, and I started to get nervous. Something wasn't right. She said she was going to get mushrooms and come right back. I was trying to figure out what could be keeping her. Two hours had now gone by since she left. She wasn't answering her phone. Nicolas came into the room and asked, "When's Mommy coming home? I'm getting hungry."

"Very soon, Nicolas," I told him. It didn't quite relieve my worries.

As I was calling Jenny's phone for the fifth time, I heard a knock at the front door. When I opened the door, a police officer stood in front of me.

"Good evening, sir. Is this the Murphy residence?" His badge read Officer Johnson.

"Yes, yes, it is. What's wrong? What happened? Where's my wife?" The blood rushing through my veins turned ice cold, and my heart moved into my throat. I began to lose control of myself as panic set in.

"Sir, please calm down. Is there someplace I can speak to you in private?" He indicated the two young children standing behind me. I hadn't noticed them standing there.

Turning to them, I told them, "Kids, go the playroom. I'll be there in a few minutes."

Nicolas, my natural-born wonderer, wouldn't do as I told him. He stood firm on his feet and asked, "But Daddy, why is the policeman here?"

Losing my temper, I screamed, "Nick, go!" I only called him Nick when he was in trouble, and it killed me to see the hurt and confusion in his eyes as he turned and ran to the playroom. Jessica followed behind him.

"Officer, please come in."

Taking his hat off, he stepped into our house. I chose the living room to talk in; it was closest to the front door. "What is it?" I asked, my voice nervous, making me sounded smaller than I was.

"Sir, I'm sorry to tell you this, but there has been an accident. Your wife is Jennifer Murphy, correct?"

I was confused over why was he calling her Jennifer. No one calls her Jennifer. "Yes, that's right. Jenny. She's my wife." My fists were jammed into the front pockets of my jeans. I found a bit of lint and rolled it between my fingers, not sure I wanted to hear what he had to say.

"It seems she was driving down Main Street when a car veered over the yellow line. Jennifer tried to avoid it and hit a tree, sir."

I was stunned and couldn't speak. It was as if someone had hit me with a tree. The room started spinning, and I found the nearest chair to catch me. My mind was juggling the details, trying to figure out how this could be happening.

"Sir, she has been airlifted to Mass General Hospital."

I looked up at Officer Johnson and I said, "So she's alive?"

"Sir, I suggest you get to the hospital. Her injuries were very severe."

After dropping the kids off with my parents, I drove to the hospital, passing cars and beeping for people to get out of my way. I called

Jenny's parents to tell them the bad news. When Bob answered, I tried to keep my voice smooth,

"Bob, it's Alex. I'm sorry to tell you this, but Jenny's been in a car accident. She's been airlifted to Boston Hospital. I'm heading there right now."

"What? Oh my God, no. What happened?"

"Bob, I'm heading in now. I will let you know when I get more information."

"No, we're heading in too. We're leaving right now. We'll see you there." *Click*: Jenny's dad had hung up.

Alone in my car, I was only halfway there. I had too much time to think, and a nauseous feeling began to expand in my stomach. "I can't lose her!" I screamed out loud. As I fought back tears, I tried to think positively and tell myself to wait until I had all the information before freaking out.

I pulled into the first parking space I saw, slammed the transmission into park, and ran to the emergency room. I was greeted by a slap in the face from the antiseptic odors of sickness. I ran to the reception desk. "Hi, I'm Alex Murphy. I was told my wife was here. Her name is Jenny Murphy. She was brought in after a car accident." My heart pounded in my chest. I couldn't believe the words that just left my mouth.

"Just a minute. Let me check on her." I stood there, my legs shaking just enough to remind me I was vulnerable. I was knocked out of control of my life. *Please be good news*, I thought.

The nurse returned to escort me to Jenny's bed. My knees buckled and I almost fell to the ground when I looked around the blue-and-white striped curtain and saw Jenny lying there. She was wrapped in bandages, with needles poking into her delicate skin; one bag of blood and another of clear fluids hung from a stand. She had a tube in her mouth. I heard the machines beep and whoosh air into her lungs.

"Oh my God. Jenny." I stood, frozen, rubbing my hands together to try to stop them from shaking. I was unsure how to get to her through all the medical equipment and wires. Her arms and face were bandaged, and very little skin was exposed enough for me to kiss her to let her know I was there.

I got the feeling the nurse had been witness to this scene many times in her career; as she left she simply said, "A doctor will be over to talk to you in a few minutes. Your wife is in a coma, but she may be able to hear you if you talk to her."

I couldn't talk to her. I was paralyzed. Standing at the footboard staring at Jenny's fragile body, I repeated in my head, *Coma?* Confused, I said under my breath, "How can this be? She was just getting mushrooms."

I sat next to the bed in the only open space available, and then I heard footsteps coming down the hall. I looked up to see Jenny's parents standing in the same place I'd stood not long before. Ann, Jenny's mother, was next to the curtain. Her mouth fell open, and I saw she was fighting to get air as her eyes focused on Jenny. "Oh, my baby. How did this happen?" Ann walked over and stood next to me at her broken daughter's bedside. Behind me, I saw Bob, his hand on Ann's shoulder, his lips pulled into his mouth, fighting back tears.

I couldn't look my mother-in-law in the eye; instead I kept staring at Jenny. "Ann, she was making me chicken marsala and didn't have mushrooms. She had already been to the store this morning, but the kids were distracting her and she forgot to get the mushrooms." I heard myself speaking but felt like I was in a fog. "I told her I would go, but she wouldn't let me. She told me I should stay home to watch the game. Damn it, it should be me in that bed, not her." I punched my fist into my palm.

A voice came from behind the curtain. "Excuse me, I'm Dr. Winters. Sorry to interrupt, but I have been observing Jennifer. Her condition is quite serious. Her head hit the windshield with great impact. The air bag did deploy, but her body was thrust above the air bag, and she hit the windshield. She has suffered major head trauma from the force of the impact."

I stood staring at Dr. Winters. He looked to be in his early thirties, and I wondered how someone so young could have enough knowledge and experience to save my wife.

"Dr. Winters, what can we do for Jenny? Will she..." I paused, not sure I was ready to hear the answer. "Make it?" I stumbled to get the words out. My tongue was so dry it felt like it was wrapped in wool.

"Time will tell. The intracranial hemorrhaging, or bleeding in the brain, should begin to decrease and show signs of receding in the next forty-eight hours. We'll be able to tell more then." He walked to the other side of Jenny's bed. "Studies have shown that sometimes patients in a comatose state can hear. I would encourage you to talk to her, let her know you're here." As he turned to leave he added, "And another thing — if you believe in the power of prayer, praying wouldn't hurt either. What I have seen people live through when they have a family that believes in prayer might astonish you. There's a chapel in the hospital, if you feel like visiting it. I'll be back to check on her." He disappeared behind the curtain.

The doctor's words were buzzing around inside my head like bees swarming a nest. *Bleeding in the brain, brain swelling, coma, forty-eight hours, talk to Jenny.* My wife was lying in a bed attached to wires and needles, bandaged from head to toe, looking for all intents and purposes dead. And he mentioned prayer. I didn't believe in prayer — that was Jenny's belief.

Jenny's mom took my hand. Looking me in the eye, she said, "Alex, we'll stay with her. Why don't you go for a walk? All of this must be so hard to take in. There is a lot to process, and I can see how upset you are."

"Thanks, Ann, I think I will. I could use some fresh air. I have my phone, so please call me if anything changes." Leaving Ann and Bob with Jenny was easy. They had both been pillars of strength for Jenny and me through the many years of our relationship.

I walked outside into the crisp, refreshing night air. I so was confused about the turn of events in our lives. Just that morning Jenny had been singing as she flipped pancakes for breakfast. Then she went to church and after that to the grocery store.

I paced on the sidewalk that surrounded the emergency room, running my hands through my hair, which felt thinner, as if it were falling out in clumps. I tried to replay the events of my day and create a different outcome. If only I had kept the kids with me instead of them going to the grocery store with her. But, Jenny had insisted on taking them with her to give me time to finish the yard work. Later, she'd been adamant about getting the mushrooms herself.

As I paced and thought about Jenny, I started to gather memories of how different she had been treating me the past six months. I was realizing that in the last year, she'd developed new ways of giving me her attention, more than determined to give me what I wanted or what she thought I wanted. Was all that time for myself, my favorite meals, the vacation of my dreams to Alaska, the endless weekend golf with my friends and my dad premeditated? I speculated she knew something I didn't; why such a sudden flip in our relationship? Did she know, could she have known, she was going to end up here and that our lives would be changed like this?

A vibration in my front pocket broke the rollercoaster of thoughts whipping around in my head.

"Hello, what happened?" I answered it.

Ann replied, "Alex, come quickly. She stopped breathing!"

I ran into the hospital. Ann and Bob were standing outside Jenny's room as I came around the corner. "What's going on?" I asked.

Bob spoke first, his voice shaky. "She was laying there just like when you left, and then everything started beeping and the nurse came running in. The doctor came and told us to step outside."

Anger erupted in my veins. "This is ridiculous! How can this be happening to her?"

Bob took hold of my arm and looked into my eyes. "Alex, breathe. She is strong, a tough girl. She'll pull through."

I wanted to believe him, but all I could say was, "I sure hope you're right, Bob. I don't know if I could live without her."

After we waited for what felt like an eternity, Dr. Winters came out of the room.

"We have stabilized her. This is common with brain trauma. It'll be a rocky road until all the swelling has decreased."

I was unsettled by Dr. Winters' manner. He seemed so matter of fact, but it was my wife fighting for her life. We were feeling helpless and numb.

"I'm going back in to see her."

As I approached my wife's hospital bed, my eyes burned and began to fill with tears. I took her motionless hand in mine. "Jenny...Jenny, if you can hear me, move your hand. Squeeze me, honey. Let me know you are in there."

Nothing happened. I stroked the small area of skin near her forehead that wasn't bandaged, pushing down the lump in my throat. I had little hope I would ever see my wife move or hear her sweet, soft voice again, the voice that possessed the power to calm me down like nothing else could.

I could feel Ann and Bob staring, watching my pathetic display of weakness playing out before them. When I turned to look at them, I couldn't tell if they looked at me with compassion or pity. I wondered how they could be so strong when their daughter was so badly wounded.

Jenny

I LOOKED AROUND; IT WAS DARK. AND THEN I NOTICED A BRIGHT-ness shining below me. When I looked into the brightness, I saw a hospital room with three people standing around the bed where a small bandaged adult lay. I was trying to put together what was happening. Confusion was growing inside me. Then I realized my husband was there. I sensed he was upset. I saw my parents standing next to him; they looked sad. Trying to figure out what was happening, I studied the person in the bed and was shocked to see that it was me. But how could I be up here and down there at the same time? While I was trying to interpret the scene playing out below, I sensed someone moving next to me. When I turned to look, I thought my eyes were playing tricks on me. I couldn't believe what I saw. A beautiful white aura in the shape of a person had replaced the darkness that had surrounded me. The aura was radiant and warm. I enjoyed the warmth; I welcomed it. It replaced my confusion with an assurance that I would be okay.

Turning to the aura, I asked, "How did I get here?" Instead of a voice, I saw and heard images. The accident flashed before eyes. I saw the other car coming at me and then my car racing toward the tree even faster before the image went blank. I heard the sound of the helicopter; people spoke quickly about blood and head injuries, and I heard the urgency in everyone's voices. I was seeing my life from above, and I didn't like it. I didn't like watching my husband and parents worry. I wanted to go to Alex and let him know I was here, I was all right, but I couldn't reach him. I hovered above, watching him and my parents in agony.

Then, the aura started to guide me. I rose and walked away from the view of the hospital room without knowing where I was going. As I walked, everything grew darker again, except for a tiny beam of light that the aura left in its wake ahead of me. It was guiding me by leaving a thin golden ray of a path for me. I could feel its warm presence as I followed the trail. Walking on the golden line, I sensed a lightness and a gentle pull forward. I kept my eyes open, hoping to see where I was heading. Off in the distance the aura's light began to grow brighter, and my vision started to come into focus. I could see all around; everywhere I looked, I saw white. I noticed a high, white fence with a beautifully adorned gold railing. The aura held me in its warmth. I was paralyzed.

As we turned around, I saw a kind of screen that was playing images of me as a young child. I was running around with my brother and parents at the beach; we were all laughing and smiling. The image changed to the day I first saw Alex at school. Oh, to see his youthful beauty again—it made me smile to recognize how long we had been together. Had it really been that long since we were kids? Then the images shifted from high school graduation to pictures of college in Michigan and my college graduation. Next, was Alex's marriage proposal and our wedding day, and then pictures of Nicolas' birth and Jessica's flashed on the screen. When I saw Nicolas as a newborn baby, despair washed over me. I wondered why I'd had to suffer through such difficult times as a new mother. Since I'd learned to accept my new life, I could now look back at those memories filled with love that I was able to experience the birth of a child. I knew I loved being a mother. I only wish I could have known that from the beginning. I know now I needed to endure those struggles to grow into the person I became.

Next I see myself sitting on a porch in a swing. The house, white with black shutters, is set back from the road, surrounded by fields and trees and flower gardens. I notice my skin has matured and my hair is white. My eyes are glued to the old lady on the swing as I notice her beauty and peaceful smile. An older man who also has white hair walks out the front door carrying a tray of glasses of lemonade. He sits down beside the older lady. Suddenly I realize it's Alex, an older but still handsome Alex. A car pulls up the long driveway. When it comes to a stop, two little kids get out and run up to the porch. I'm confused; they're not Nicolas or Jessica, but I see resemblances. A beautiful woman emerges from behind the driver's seat, and she waves in our direction. She walks up to the porch. I recognize Jessica. I realize that those must be her children. I see the joyful expression on older Jenny's face as she turns to Alex, and he smiles at her. And then the image is gone.

As the images fade from the younger Jenny to an older Jenny, I cry out not to be taken from my blissful memories. I turned around, looking for someone or for some direction. The movie ended all too soon, and I don't know which way to walk or what I should do, so I just stand there.

Alex

I SAT BY JENNY'S BEDSIDE ALL NIGHT, WAITING FOR HER TO WAKE UP, to talk or squeeze my hand, but there were no changes overnight. I encouraged Jenny's parents to leave and go home to sleep. I knew I would need them for support the next day. My parents kept Nicolas and Jessica at their house overnight and promised to get them to school in the morning. They were careful not tell them how severe their mother's accident was; we didn't need to cause them any more stress than they were feeling after the sudden changes to their family.

By morning I became increasingly anxious that Jenny wouldn't come back to me. As the nursing staff switched shifts, I stepped outside to get fresh air and try to clear the feelings of lost hope and my belief Jenny wouldn't wake up. I expected that seeing healthy people moving about would reassure me that my life would return to normal and I would leave this hospital with my wife, the same wife I woke up with yesterday morning, healthy and full of life.

As nurses and doctors shuffled in and out of the hospital, I sat at the curb. More than eighteen hours had passed since the accident. Overnight, Jenny's heart had stopped for the second time, reminding me how helpless I felt. Everything was out of my control. It was a new feeling for me. I had always been in control of my life and got out of it exactly what I wanted. In every situation, I was the one who made sure everyone in my family was taken care of, but in this situation there was nothing that I could do but wait. The loss of control just about killed me.

The cool October morning air had a bite to it. I began to shiver. I'd left the house without taking a jacket; I was wearing just a t-shirt and jeans. I decided taking a walk inside the hospital would be warmer.

Wandering through the halls, I was struck by the many levels of care taking place in one building. Some people came in for laboratory tests, others for emergency care. On other levels patients were recovering from operations. Then I noticed the sign for labor and delivery. It seemed odd that in one building, patients could die on one floor and yet two floors up a new mother welcomed a newborn baby into the world. Sadness and sorrow below, joy and elation above.

As I walked the halls considering the different outcomes that could potentially happen in one building, something stopped me in my tracks. I realized I was standing in front of the door to the chapel. I felt an overwhelming desire to enter, which struck me as odd. I was not a praying man or a faith-filled man. Faith was Jenny's thing. I got through life on my own terms and under my own control. But as I stood before the doorway, I felt a sudden stirring inside me — something was drawing me in. "God, you have brought me here, haven't you?" I reached for the doorknob and entered the chapel.

I noticed how small it was. It was peacefully dim. Chairs were lined up in four rows on each side. An altar rose at the back of the room. Artificial silk trees and real flowers were set around the room. I was thankful to that see I was alone. I took a seat in the front row next to the aisle. Letting the weight of my head rest in my hands, I started talking, "Dear God, I'm not usually a praying man. I don't know how to do this. Jenny always wanted to bring me to church and to build a stronger faith together, but I wasn't into it. She was the one who kept our family in her prayers. She always turned to prayer when her life went out of balance, and she would remark about how centered she felt after she took a few minutes to talk to you. Lord, help her. She needs prayers for herself now. She has been terribly injured. I can't help her, but I can hear her voice echoing in my head — all things are possible with God. Please, Lord, help her."

I looked up to the ceiling, surprised to feel so comfortable. I continued, "God, please make Jenny wake up. Take away the brain swelling. Help her to recover so we can be a family again." I sat there for a while, surrounded by the peace the room offered. I realized how tired I was. It had been a long night. I needed to keep moving or I was sure I would fall asleep right there in chapel. I rose from my seat, and as I turned to walk to the door, I made a promise out loud. "God, I will be back."

In what seemed like no time, I was back in the intensive care unit, feeling a little more hopeful after my visit to the chapel. I never realized how sitting and praying in silence could bring a peaceful feeling to one's spirit.

I heard voices as I came around the corner toward Jenny's room. As I entered, I saw my parents sitting by Jenny's bed. My mother got up and embraced me with tears in her eyes. "Alex, I'm so sorry this happened." My dad, never a man for showing much emotion, simply patted my back. I could tell he had been crying because his eyes were red.

I wasn't sure if my parents understood Jenny's condition, so I shared all I knew, which wasn't enough. "The doctors don't know more than they did yesterday. She's flat-lined and been brought back twice." I tried to lighten the mood. "I keep waiting for her to wake up and make a silly joke about all this." As I stared at my wife's motionless body, I felt whatever hope the chapel had offered lose its power to the voice of defeat in my mind.

"Alex, you need to be strong for her. Keep your energy high; she'll sense it. She'll come out of this okay." My mother's faith was even stronger than Jenny's. I wondered why I lacked the faith that my mother carried so proudly and had shown me my whole life. All that I could try to do was to learn to believe that something bigger than me was in control of the drastic changes happening in my life. I couldn't change overnight after believing I had been in control my whole life.

We stood shoulder to shoulder, looking at Jenny. "I don't know, Mom. I don't know what to do here. It's killing me to see her like this. It should be me there in that bed, not her. She is so small and fragile." My voiced cracked like a dried-up nutshell as I fought back tears. My mother took my hand in hers and squeezed it. I felt her love and support through the simple gesture.

"Have you eaten, Alex?" My dad stood by my other side. "Let's go find the cafeteria and get some breakfast. We'll leave your mom to stay with Jenny. What do you say — are you hungry?"

My stomach growled at the thought of food. I hadn't eaten since lunchtime yesterday. I didn't have an appetite, though. It had been replaced with a gnawing, churning sensation in my stomach. The thought of adding food to it made my throat close up and caused me to gag. I wondered when I would want to eat again. I knew I needed to eat to stoke my energy. Overruling the nausea, I agreed. "Yeah, Dad, let's get something to eat."

I turned back to my mother and told her, "Keep your eyes on her. Please call me if there are any changes."

"I will. Go with Dad and take a break from this tiresome room. Have some food. Maybe being in a new setting will help you see clearer." She kissed my cheek and then sat in the chair next to Jenny's bed.

Jenny

AFTER WATCHING THE IMAGES OF MY LIFE PLAY OUT IN FRONT OF me, I found myself looking down into the hospital room, the aura by my side. I felt renewed. From above I could see and hear everything my family and the medical staff said, but I couldn't speak or move. I watched helplessly; I knew what they didn't. The images gave me faith I was going to live. I'd come close to dying, but my close call with death had given me a magical gift. The scenes of my life I'd witnessed let me know I would live a full life. I would be a grandmother some-day.

Watching everyone in the hospital room was eerie. They didn't realize that my soul—not my body in the bed, but my soul—could see and hear everything. I wished they could know what I'd seen. If they knew what I knew, I wouldn't have to see my husband so dis-traught. I was happy to hear my father-in-law offer to get breakfast with Alex—he needed to eat to keep up his energy.

My mother-in-law, Mary, stayed to watch over me. I heard her whispered prayers. I felt even more warmth begin to surround me, coming from the prayers my mother-in-law was offering. She was speaking life into my body, and it was responding. After she prayed, she began talking to me as if I were awake. I listened to her tell me how my children were doing. I had never doubted my mother-in-law would take good care of them. She was filled with amazing amounts of love for her grandchildren and showed them both how special they were to her.

Mary sat next to my bed holding my hand in hers, stroking it gently as she spoke. She told me what Nicolas and Jessica ate for dinner, what time they went to bed, what they had for breakfast. She reported that they went to school, but they really wanted to see their mother.

Mary continued talking, holding my hand and rubbing the back of it. I wasn't sure she felt me squeeze her hand; it was subtle at first. Mary told me she and Tom were picking the kids up from school and they would take them to their activities. Then she told me that she wanted me to get well. Feeling the strength from all the warmth around me, I needed to let her know I could hear her. I kept trying to squeeze her hand, but I couldn't do it hard enough for her to feel it.

"Jenny, we all love you, and we know you are strong. I've been praying for you, darling. You have so much life left to live. Please, Jenny, don't give up. We all are here for you."

I needed to let her know that I could hear her, but it was so hard to move my body. My hands felt like they were stuck in concrete. The more I tried to squeeze, the less I succeeded. I looked at the aura next to me and asked with frustration, "Why can't I move? I need to let her know…I need to let her know I'm here."

I demanded that the aura allow me to squeeze my mother-in-law's hand. When I tried again, I tightened my hand around hers a little more strongly. I knew the sensation was evident; I knew Mary felt my hand tighten around her hand.

Mary must have been feeling confused, not sure if she really felt what she thought she did. She said to me, "If you can hear me, Jenny, squeeze my hand again." This time, with more determination, I put all my strength into it and squeezed as hard as I could. She felt it. Adrenaline must have rushed through her veins. She cried, "Jenny, you can hear me! You can hear me! I need to get the doctor."

She called the nurse's station on the controller. "Nurse, she squeezed my hand! Jenny squeezed my hand!"

I heard the nurse respond, "I'll get the doctor."

Within minutes the doctor was by my bedside checking me over. "This is a good sign. Keep talking to her — I think she can hear you."

When the doctor left, Mary began praying for me again, this time prayers of thanks for feeling me squeeze her hand.

Alex

AFTER FEEDING MY NERVOUS STOMACH, I TOLD MY FATHER, "DAD, there's somewhere I need to go before we head back to see Jenny. Will you come with me?"

We left the cafeteria and stopped at the chapel door. My dad looked confused.

"You want to go in there. You?"

"There is no one more surprised than I am, Dad. I was here earlier this morning, and the difference in how I felt going in and coming out was amazing. Somehow I was more peaceful."

Touching my shoulder, my father said, "It's a good thing, son. Your mother will be proud. Let's go in and pray for Jenny."

Earlier, the atmosphere in Jenny's hospital room had felt stale and heavy, but when I walked back in the air seemed to have been replaced with a fresh new lightness that was strong against the darkness that was trying to take back the hold it once had on the room.

I heard my mother speaking from the chair next to Jenny's bed. As my father and I walked in, my mother jumped up and said, "Alex, I'm so glad you're here. I tried to call, but I couldn't through to your phone."

"What is it, Mom?" I rushed to Jenny's bedside.

A smile beamed from her face. "Honey, she moved. Jenny moved her hand." My mother was smiling from ear to ear.

I looked from Jenny to my mother. "What? What do you mean?"

My mother explained. "I began to pray for her, and then I talked to her about the children and told her what we did with them and about our after-school plans. I thought I felt her move her hand, but I wasn't sure. I told her to do it again, and the second time I felt her gently tighten her fingers around mine. I called for the doctor. He said it was a good sign and we should keep talking to her. Alex, I think she's going to make it."

I picked up Jenny's hand. "Jenny, can you hear me? Jenny, honey, it's me, Alex. I'm here. Please squeeze my hand. Please, honey, just a little. Let me know you can hear me." But nothing happened. I turned to my mother, feeling empty. "I didn't feel anything. Nothing happened. She didn't do it." I was fooling myself to think it could happen as easy that, but I was reaching for anything that revealed that life remained in Jenny's body.

"We'll leave you alone. Just keep talking to her. Tell her stories. When she's ready, she'll do it again. Keep faith, Alex." My parents hugged me and then gave me privacy with Jenny.

I found being alone with her felt strange. I expected too much from her. I needed to feel her move, to know she could hear me like she heard my mother. I started talking to her, but it felt like I was talking to myself because no one answered me. As I sat by Jenny's bed, I recalled the first time I saw her. Resting my head on her bed, I closed my eyes so I could see the teenage image of Jenny. "Oh, Jenny, you were so beautiful. You came out of nowhere into my life. With that one look at you, I knew I would never be the same. I hadn't seen you around school before that day in cafeteria, but once I did, I couldn't forget you." Stroking her arm, I watched for the goose bumps that always came in the wake of my touch, but nothing. I kept talking, hoping my words would give her the strength to squeeze my hand. "I spent my days looking for you. I would walk into class, hoping to see you there, wishing you had transferred in. Searching for you in the halls between classes, I felt like I had eyes all over my head. Oh, I remember one time I did see you. I don't think you saw me though. You were standing against the lockers talking to your friends. Someone must have said something to make you laugh. Your face lit up. I swear I saw your eyes twinkle." I held her hand in mine, rubbing it, while I told her how crazy I was about her in the early days of our love.

"I remember my teammates were mad at me because I lost my focus and I couldn't run drills. It was crazy! I truly believe it was love at first sight. No one had ever made me feel like you did. No one has since then, and no one ever will. There is not one other woman out there who will make me feel like you do." I stopped and waited to see if she would respond, but I didn't feel anything. I only heard the sounds coming from the machines that were keeping her alive. "Jenny, my sweet angel, please come back to us. I can't stand living one day without hearing your sweet voice or seeing your smile. You are my love. You will always be my one and only."

Jenny

HOVERING ABOVE THE HOSPITAL ROOM, I FELT WATER DRIP ON MY hand. I realized tears were running down my face. Alex's words were slipping their way into my heart. Every word he spoke soothed my aching body and brought me closer to knowing I could survive this accident.

We had always shared our feelings for each other. When we were with other people and unable to speak about how we were feeling, we would wink at each other to show each other our love. But now, lying in bed, unable to speak, I felt helpless. I knew he loved me, but hearing him tell me while I was unable to talk to him and to tell him in return how much I loved him was different. I wanted to talk to him, to hug him, to let him know I was all right. I was full of deep love and admiration for my family, for them coming to see me and telling me how much they loved me and wanted me to get better.

Even though my accident was a terrible experience for us all, I was given the gift of hearing my family speak about how special I was and how my life mattered to them, the people who were most important to me. I had a stronger determination to live, but I knew returning to my old life would take time. I was still too weak.

Alex

ANGER GREW INSIDE AS I THOUGHT ABOUT HOW POWERLESS I WAS while the woman I loved fought for her life. "Jenny, I need you to fight. You're not a quitter. You're a fighter, Jenny." Then it happened and stopped my thoughts. I stopped talking. I felt it—it wasn't strong, but she squeezed my fingers. "Jenny! Jenny, I felt it. You can hear me! Oh, honey, I love you." My tears landed on her bandaged head, and I kissed her everywhere I could find her bare, delicate skin. I left a kiss to show her I was there and that I loved her.

While I sat in silence, hospital sounds in the background, I began to pray to God. I thanked him for the bit of hope in my heart. Soon my parents and Jenny's parents returned to the room and stood at the foot of Jenny's bed. I told them that Jenny squeezed my hand when I told her to come back to me, and they were all filled with joy. I saw my mother and Ann's tears fall. It was a great day of progress for Jenny, and our family felt renewed hope in their hearts.

Ann stood next to me near the bed, holding my hand, filled with optimism. "Alex, she had a good day today. I believe she will come out of this." Jenny's mom was right—it was a good day, a step in the right direction.

The nurse came to take Jenny away for more tests to see if the swelling had decreased since the accident. I walked our parents to their cars for some fresh air.

"We'll be back early tomorrow." Ann hugged me.

"Take care of yourself, Alex. Please try to get some sleep." Bob shook my hand.

"Thank you for all your help today. I'll try to sleep tonight."

After seeing my parents to their car and thanking them for picking up my children from school, I visited the chapel for the third time that day before returning to Jenny's room.

Sitting in the front of the chapel, I thought it was odd that more people didn't come seeking the comfort this room held. Maybe I had walked among more nonbelievers than I ever realized, but I was changed now. I was becoming a believer in a higher power; things were changing in my life, and I was learning I wasn't in control of any of it.

I spoke out loud this time. "Well, it seems I've been a fool all these years. I've shut you out of my life, thinking I was in charge and in control. Jenny tried to tell me over and over about the power that prayer holds. She told me that You would give me what I need, not what I want. I'm just angry it had to take this accident and my wife almost being killed to teach me I'm not in control. God, I pray for Jenny's recovery, and I pray she is healed from her injuries. Please, Lord, help me and Jenny and our families."

Jenny was brought back to her room after I finished in the chapel, and the nurse said the test results would be available in a couple of hours. With some renewed hope, I took a seat next to the bed. I knew it would be a long night; I wasn't expecting any more visitors. I had to eat dinner, and I needed to talk to Nicolas and Jessica. I hadn't talked to them since Jenny was in the accident. I looked up at the clock; it was ten of five, and they should almost be home from their activities. I told Jenny I hated to leave her alone, but I knew our children needed to hear my voice, and I needed to hear about life outside of this institution.

"I'm going to call the kids and get something to eat. I'll be back soon. Rest, darling. I love you."

I stood watching Jenny's unconscious body for a few minutes, noticing the rhythmic rise and fall of her chest. How peaceful and calm she looked. I wondered if she knew what was happening to her. Would she remember any of this? Time would tell.

"Hey, big guy, it's Daddy," I said to Nicolas. "How was school?" I stood outside, enjoying the crisp nighttime air, which was revitalizing after being in the hospital most of the day.

"We had gym class today. I threw the ball the farthest, and we got to run around the track like the big kids. It was so cool." His words were electrified.

"That's great, buddy. How was soccer practice?"

"Good. We ran drills and had a scrimmage against the other twelve-and-under team." The electricity faded. He asked, "How's Mommy?"

"Oh, bud, she's getting better. She has a really bad headache, but the doctors are giving her medicine for it, so she's not in any pain. Your mom's a strong lady, but she will need to stay in the hospital until the doctor gives her all the medicine her body needs to get better. Do you understand, Nicolas? "

"Daddy, when is she coming home?"

"Well, it's hard to say for sure. I guess when they are done giving her the medicine. It could be a couple weeks, buddy. You and Jessica will stay at Mimi and Papa's. They are going to take good care of you. I'll come to see you guys as soon as I can. It's hard to leave Mommy because she needs me here, Nicolas."

"Okay, Daddy. I miss both of you. Please take good care of her." The heaviness in his little-boy voice just about broke my heart. *He shouldn't have to be going through this*, I thought.

"I will take great care of her, Nicolas, don't you worry about that. Can you to help me by taking care of yourself and your sister until we are all together again?"

"Sure, Dad, I can try."

"Is your sister there?"

Jessica came on the phone. "Hi, Daddy."

"Oh, hi, sweetie." Hearing her sweet, innocent voice on the telephone always reminded me of how young she was. Although she loved wearing Jenny's high heels and lipstick and spending hours dressing and acting like a big girl, I knew that at eight, Jessica was still a young girl.

Not missing a beat she asked, "Is Mommy coming home soon?"

Hearing her ask with such desperation hit me hard. "Well, sweetie, she needs to take her medicine at the hospital. The doctors will tell us when she can leave and come home. It might a couple weeks, honey."

I heard her start to whimper.

"Oh, honey, don't cry. Momma's going to be better very soon. Her body is working really hard to feel better." How could I explain why my young daughter's mother was unable to be at home with her and do so in a way she could understand? "Do you remember last winter when you had a fever and Mommy gave you medicine for it?"

Her soft voice broke the silence that was pouring through the phone line. "Yeah."

"You see, Mommy has a really bad headache, and the doctors are giving her medicine, so she can feel better. Just like she helped you feel better, the doctors are helping her feel better. We need to give the doctors and nurses time to take Mommy's boo-boo away. So please don't cry. Everything will be okay. Mommy loves you and Nicolas so much, she wouldn't want either of you to be sad."

"But Daddy, I miss you guys. It's not the same without you here."

As I heard her begin to whimper again, I had to close my eyes to stop from imagining Jessica crying. It was tearing me up inside to hear how Jenny's accident hurt the kids.

"Sweetie, I will come see you real soon, as soon as Mommy's medicine makes her feel better." I felt helpless, unable to hold Jessica and help her feel safe. "I know — maybe Mimi can cuddle you real tight tonight and read you an extra story. I know how much you love story time. What do you say to that?"

"Yeah, I like that. I'm going to pick my books right now." I noticed a lightness return to her voice that filled me with hope that perhaps I had soothed her worries for now.

I hated to hang up, but my stomach was telling me I needed to grab dinner. I also wanted to get back to Jenny. "I'll call you again tomorrow. Have a good night. Sweet dreams. I love you very much."

"I love you too, Daddy."

I waited on the line until I heard her hang up. Leaning against the wall of the hospital, I took a deep breath. As I blew it out, I noticed the vapor spin in circles as it left my mouth. The night air was setting in with a bitter chill. Although I felt content knowing my children were safe with my parents at home, another part of me was still numb. I didn't know how well Jenny would ever be or even if she would wake up again. As my fears grew, the wind whipped through the passageway where I was standing and forced me to move inside. At least the heat in the hospital could take the chill from my bones. If I was lucky, maybe being warm would take away my worries for the moment.

I sat alone at a table in the corner of the cafeteria and looked down at the tray full of food. The aroma of the chicken pot pie and mashed potatoes made my mouth water, and the slice of apple pie reminded of the pies my mother made in the fall. I took my first bite. It felt good to eat; the flavors melded together and satisfied my hunger. Food would give me energy, and that's all I really cared about.

After my dinner, I drank a cup of coffee as I finished the pie, thinking of stories I could tell Jenny that night. I wanted stories to share about our love and the way I felt when I was around her that she had never heard before. As I sat thinking about possibilities, I felt a tap on my shoulder. I turned to see Dr. Winters standing over me, carrying a tray of food.

"May I join you?"

I was surprised that the doctor ate in the cafeteria with patients' families and other hospital faculty. I thought he would have eaten in his office. I was happy to have company. "Sure, have a seat."

"You look like you are doing some deep thinking. I don't want to interrupt you."

"Oh, no — it's okay. Please sit. I was thinking about Jenny."

"Ah, I see. That's what I thought."

"I find myself thinking about everything that's happened. I just never thought something like this would happen to either of us, you know? This stuff happens to other people and other families. I wasn't prepared for something like this."

"I hear that a lot. No one is ready for these things, but you learn as you go. You're handling it very well." He sat and picked up his fork.

I looked down at his tray of food and noticed he was eating the same meal I ordered. *It must be the perfect fall night for chicken pot pie.*

"Ya' think?" I asked, surprised.

"Well, you're here. I can't say that for all the families of the patients I have treated. It would surprise you how many patients are alone in here."

"I wouldn't want to be anywhere else. I need to be here, by her side. You know, this all happened because she went to the store to get mushrooms for my dinner. I mean, did the meal really need mushrooms? I didn't need mushrooms. I'm sure dinner would have tasted fine without them." I watched as steam escaped from the coffee cup. "I guess I feel a lot of guilt about what happened to her."

"You shouldn't feel any guilt, Alex. A driver was out of control, and unfortunately your wife was the one who suffered. You played no part in that. I will tell you that talking is good. You need to release your thoughts and emotions. It helps to hear yourself speak about how you feel. You need to let others help you too. This is a process that affects the family just as much as the patient. I would encourage you to keep talking it out with friends and family. You'll start to realize that you are not responsible for your wife's condition and that no one is ready for this — no one sees it coming, but somehow we make it through, no matter what the outcome is."

"Thanks, Dr. Winters. After I survive this, I guess I'll be more prepared for the next incident. I've got to admit I've been pretty lucky in life. This is the first time something tragic has happened to me."

"Alex, I wouldn't say you're lucky. I would consider you blessed." He locked eyes with me.

I sat quietly and let the doctor enjoy his dinner. I contemplated the differences between being lucky and being blessed. I began to think that luck is when a person takes chances and has a good outcome. But being blessed means having a belief in a higher power and trusting that it knows exactly what a person needs in life. Everything that happens to that person happens for a purpose, not just by accident.

"I never thought of it like that before. I think I'm learning a lot from this accident." After all the years Jenny had shared her thoughts about spirituality, I was at a point where I could see how life was affecting me, pushing me to grow, and I could feel the presence of a higher power. I never would have thought I could believe like Jenny or my mother, but here I sit, pondering the thought that I once believed I had control over my life. *I might not be in control of my life, but I have been blessed to live the life I have.*

"Let's go check on the patient. What do you think?" Dr. Winter stood.

His voice broke into my contemplations. I'd spent enough time thinking deep, heavy thoughts, and I agreed to go to Jenny.

As nighttime ticked along, and I prepared myself for sleep, I was glad I'd picked up a toothbrush and some toothpaste from the gift shop. I stared at myself in the mirror while I brushed my teeth, feeling love about the thought of the stories I would tell Jenny tonight.

I pulled my chair up next to Jenny's bed and started my first story, holding her hand in mine, hoping I would feel her move again. "Jenny, there have been times in my life when I thought I'd go mad without you. The summer between our junior and senior year at college was the first time I remember missing you so much at bedtime that I could barely sleep. I had gotten so used to sleeping next to you during the school year that when I went home, I couldn't sleep through the night without waking and thinking about you. It drove me crazy! The fact was I slept better with you next to me.

"So I got the idea to put two pillows next to me, so it would feel like you were there and I could sleep better. It wasn't as good as having your body next to me, but it seemed to help. In the morning when I woke up, I couldn't wait to see you, but my mom always wanted to make me breakfast. I would eat as fast as I could and then race to get to your house." I traced her knuckles.

"One day I got to your house and your mom said you had already left. You had gone out running with your dad. I felt bummed out. When I wasn't with you, I felt incomplete, and I hated feeling that I needed to have you by my side."

Being dependent on Jenny to satisfy my loneliness made me feel weak. Any free time I had was spent with Jenny, and if she wasn't available to be with me, I didn't know what to do with myself. During the early years in college, we spent every free minute together. When we returned home for the summer it was hard for me to be away from her.

"Jenny, when you came into my life, everything changed. Before you, I had sports, school, and my friends, in that order, and I felt good about my life. I didn't need anything more because I didn't know what more I could have. Then I met you and everything shifted. Not in a bad way; it just happened. Any time I wasn't playing hockey or lacrosse, all I wanted was to be with you. You came into my life and filled me with love. Jenny, I couldn't imagine a life without you, then or now."

I stared at Jenny, hoping to feel her squeeze my hand or see movement in her bandaged body, but nothing happened. I looked at her bruises, dark shades of purple, and I was troubled that my wife, the love of my life, the person I would do anything to protect, was so badly injured. I shook my head and continued with my next story, hoping to lighten my mood.

"This next one is good. I know you'll remember it…Do you remember the time we went to the holiday party at college our senior year? Oh, my goodness, I'll never forget it. You went crazy thinking about what you were going to wear and how your hair was going to look. I was content going in jeans and a sweater, but no way—you wanted me in a suit. By that time, I had my old car at school. It was a beater but still running okay—or so I thought. I picked you up from your apartment, and you looked amazing. You took my breath away when you opened the door. You wore a sparkly red dress and your hair was up. It had some curls, I think. When we walked down the stairs, you were being very careful not to trip over your dress and put a hole in it with your heel. As we got to the car and I opened the door for you, we noticed snowflakes falling from the sky. You were so excited. You thought having a snowstorm during the party made the night more festive. We shared a quick kiss before I helped you in the car and closed the door.

"If I remember it right, we were about one mile away from the hotel where the dance was being held when I noticed smoke pouring out from under the hood. I pulled over to check it out, in my suit no less. The storm had picked up. The winds began blowing the snow sideways. I could barely see my hand in front of my face as I opened the hood. Smoke poured out all over me, like a chimney, and I started to cough and fan the smoke away. I reeked like smoke when I got back in the car. We were stranded.

"I looked at you sitting in the car, so beautiful, and I was about to ruin all of it. You had worked so hard that day to transform yourself for the party. I felt terrible to have to tell you we had no other choice but to walk the rest of the way to the party." I laughed out loud, recalling how we'd looked when we finally arrived at the party. "I can remember the look on our friends' faces when we walked in the function hall looking like snow people. Your hair was almost all covered in snow;

your dress was soaked half way up. It was a good thing you wore a jacket to keep the top dry. My suit was soaked, my hair looked as bad as yours, and my feet were freezing. Everyone stared at us like we were aliens. No one said a thing until good old James Bergeron yelled out in a drunken voice, 'Hey, check out the freaks,' and everyone laughed at us." I started to laugh harder, thinking what a sight we must have been.

Remembering all the things Jenny and I had experienced together and thinking I could lose her now because of the car accident made me sad. "Jenny, that was so long ago, and we didn't know what waited ahead for us, but now we have been through so much more together. You're everything to me and part of all of my favorite memories. For every choice I have made in life, I thought first about how it would affect you. You're the first thing I think about when I wake up and the last thing before I fall asleep. I'm not ready to lose you, Jenny Murphy. If you can hear me, you better come back to me and to our children. I spoke with them today. They miss you and want you to come home soon. If anyone can beat this, you can. You are strong, you're my rock, and I need you." I looked at her small and delicate hand and kissed the back of it. "I love you, Jenny. Good night, darling. Sweet dreams."

Exhausted, I pushed the chair away from the bed and fetched the pillow and the blanket the nurse left for me. I reclined the chair and closed my eyes, feeling a loss because I was unable to reach her to-night with my stories. I'd had high hopes she would squeeze my hand again, to let me know she could hear me. I knew I would have a hard time trying to fall asleep, even though I was tired and needed the rest. The machines that kept Jenny alive beeped and clicked on and off every few minutes, a soundtrack to my irrational thoughts.

Jenny

I WATCHED FROM ABOVE AS MY HUSBAND TRIED TO KEEP IT TO-gether. I wanted so badly to return to him, but it was too hard to move and I was so tired. My limbs felt as heavy as cinderblocks. It took all my strength to tighten my hand around my mother-in-law and Alex's hands earlier that day, and there was no way I could have squeezed Alex's hand tonight, even though I was desperate to. I wanted to tell him I could hear him and that I remembered the story. He left out that I had to walk in five inches of snow wearing high heels! At least he'd worn shoes that protected his feet from the cold snow.

Above the hospital room, I thought about what Alex said about going through so much together. I wondered if he remembered our first year of college and how hard it was to be away from each other. My mind wandered back to the day Alex left to go to college. When he did, the life I knew went with him.

"I'll call you every day, Jenny." I was in Alex's arms and we were hugging each other. Alex would be leaving in the morning with his parents to drive out to Michigan.

"Alex, it will be weird not having you here."

"We'll be fine." Alex had pulled away and stared into my eyes.

I wasn't sure we would be fine. I thought he would be fine because he would have distraction, but I knew I would be miserable without him.

"Alex, I wish I was going with you." That's when I started to think that I had made a mistake by not accepting the offer to attend Michigan State. If I had, I could be leaving with him that day, instead of staying home without him.

"Jenny," he said, taking hold of my hands, "you'll be busy with school. The time will go by faster than you think."

"But I'll miss your games." Tears were building behind my eyes.

"I'll call you after every one and fill you in." He took my face in his hands and wiped my tears away with his thumbs, drying the tears as they fell, leaving a warm streak where his skin touched mine.

I took a deep breath. I knew I shouldn't be acting like this; it had to be hard for him too, and I wasn't helping matters. "I'm sorry I'm being a baby, Alex. It must be hard for you, leaving your friends and parents."

"Don't apologize. You're allowed to have emotions." He smiled at me. "I feel okay about leaving my family and friends — it's you I'm going to miss and worry about the most."

"I love you, Alex," I said, holding him tight.

"I love you too, Jenny, and I always will."

I remember the walk to the front door was too short. The last thing I wanted was to say good-bye to him. I had been dreading it all summer. "Call me when you get there."

"It will be the first thing I do. Good-bye, Jenny."

"Good-bye, Alex. I'll miss you."

I blinked my eyes, and when I opened them Alex was below me, asleep in the chair next to my bed. I missed him now like I'd missed him when he was at college. I didn't like the separation between us. I knew I would have to fight to get back to him, just like I did before.

By Christmas of our first semester of college, I had been desperate to see Alex. He had been unable to come home for Thanksgiving because of his hockey commitment, and his Christmas break would be shorter than mine because he needed to be at games and practices, but at least he was coming home.

Fifteen minutes before, the clock had chimed three. He should have been there by three. I was anxious as I sat waiting at the window on Christmas Eve. The first part of the school year was harder on me than it had been for Alex. He was busy with schoolwork and hockey, and he was meeting new people and enjoying campus life. We spoke every day, but it wasn't the same as being together. I could always hear girls in the background when we talked on the phone, and I wondered what they were doing there. Insecure, I imagined the things the girls were trying to get Alex's attention. He explained that they were in the TV room, and he didn't even know who they were. The phone in his dorm room was broken, and without a phone on every level, kids waited in the TV room to call home.

My worries were interrupted when his car pulled into my parents' driveway. I opened the door and ran out to greet him.

"Alex!"

"Hey there, you. Oh, I missed you, Jenny."

We hugged in the driveway. I didn't want to let go; it felt like a dream to be in his arms again. I had spent too many months away from him, trying to remember how it felt to be in his arms, and now that he was here, I wasn't letting go yet.

"Well, can I come in?"

"Yes. Yes, I'm sorry. Let's go in."

As we walked to the house, I held tight to his hand, and he tightened his fingers around my hand and smiled at me. Butterflies fluttered in my stomach. I had missed him too much.

My mom had decorated the house with all our holiday decorations, and Alex noticed. "It looks great in here." He studied the village under the Christmas tree and the carolers standing upright on the mantel, heads tilted and mouths open. Turning to me he said, "I love the holidays."

"Me too. I especially love having you here." I rose on my tippy toes and planted a kiss on his cheek.

Besides the strong desire to be with him, nothing felt different between us as I stood next to Alex. It was as if he hadn't been away for four months. He looked good. His hair was longer than usual but still stylish. From what I could see and feel over his clothes, his body seemed even more toned than before he left. I liked feeling his strong arm muscles through his sweater as we stood looking at the Christmas tree. As I touched his arm, I felt a sudden urge to bring him upstairs.

"Where are you taking me, Jenny?"

"Well, I have to show you something upstairs. It's a…it's a gift, a Christmas gift."

"Oh, yours is at my parents' house. I didn't know if I should bring it or not."

"We can save it for later. I have to give you this one now. My parents are out picking up the food for tonight's party. We have about an hour before they come home."

As we approached my room, I saw a smile grow on Alex's face. "Oh, I think I'm going to like this gift."

I opened the door and headed to my radio to find a station that played love songs. When I turned around, Alex had already taken his shirt off. I was right about his muscles. His shoulders were wider, his biceps defined, and his stomach muscles rippled like the ocean floor after high tide.

We met each other halfway. He reached for my shirt and pulled it over my head. He lifted my chin and looked into my eyes. "Jenny, I've missed you so much." But before I could speak, his lips were on mine and I felt his tongue tickle my tongue. More butterflies raced in my stomach. I'd missed him even more than I thought. As we lay down on top of my bed, I was glad for an hour of alone time with Alex. We made every minute of it count.

Alex stirred in his chair and returned me back to the reality of my life. Sunlight broke through the blackness that nighttime spread. I looked down to see Alex waking as another day was starting. I prayed that maybe this would be the one when I woke up.

Alex

I STRETCHED MY ARMS OVER MY HEAD, TRYING TO UNDO THE STIFF-
ness in my muscles from sleeping in the convertible chair. There was
no use trying to sleep any longer; the rising sun lit the room and cast a
yellow hue all around. The hospital didn't have the best window
shades, but then again most patients weren't there to sleep.

Before draining my bladder in the bathroom, I went to check on
Jenny. Hoping she could hear me, I said to her, "Good morning, Sunshine. How did you sleep?" I didn't get a response, but there was all day
for her to make progress. I tried to keep my thoughts positive.

"My bed was pretty stiff. Man, I can't wait to get you out of here
and bring you back home to sleep in our own bed. It's much more
comfortable."

It appeared to me Jenny that hadn't made any progress during the
night. She looked content though, so I headed out for breakfast, knowing that I needed food to keep up my energy to handle whatever situation might unfold today.

I was becoming quite used to the food in the cafeteria, and it's
pretty hard to mess up eggs and bacon. As I sat taking bites of my
breakfast, I remembered last night with Jenny and the stories I told her.
I began to question if she heard me or knew if I was there.

While I was worrying about whether Jenny would ever wake up or
be normal again, I looked up from my plate and was shocked to see a
priest in line ordering breakfast. I couldn't believe it—was it a sign? I
believed it was. It was all I had at the moment, so I prayed silently.

"Please, Lord, hear me. Please help Jenny get better. She needs you now, and I need you too."

Gazing at the holy man, I asked God, "Give me a sign, Lord. I want to know if Jenny can hear me. Show me anything—I'll take anything. I just need to know she is going to be okay." I left it at that. I knew it wouldn't happen right away, but I put all my faith into that prayer and waited for the sign to come, believing God was watching over us. I was beaming with faith, knowing that today Jenny was going to show signs she could hear what was going on around her.

Before I returned to Jenny, I called to say good morning to my children. "Hey, guys. Good morning."

"Daddy!"

"I wanted to tell you that your mom had a great sleep and is ready to start another day. She is working really hard to get strong and come home. Hey, did you guys pray for your mom today?"

"I didn't." Nicolas answered first.

"Not me."

"Well, let's pray together now." I felt a bit uncomfortable. I had never prayed with my children before. Jenny always handled prayer time. I wondered if they could hear the nervousness in my voice.

"Daddy, you pray?" Nicolas sounded as shocked as I felt.

"I have learned about prayer since Mommy has been in the hospital, Nicolas. So now I'm trying to pray for Mommy."

"Okay, Daddy."

Short and sweet, I told myself. Then I took a deep breath, and said, "Please, Lord, help Mommy get better real soon. Now you guys say, Amen.'

"Amen." Nicolas sounded very serious.

"Amen." Jessica's voice was softer.

"I hope you guys have a great day at school. I love you and miss you."

The reply came to me in unison: "You too, Daddy."

I walked into Jenny's room as Rita was checking Jenny's vitals.

"Good morning, Alex. Was the chair bed comfortable for you?"

"Well, it wasn't like sleeping at home, but it served the purpose. Thank you." I took my position next to Jenny's bed. "How is the patient today?"

"Her vitals seem stronger than yesterday. The doctor will probably look into ordering more tests to see how she is recovering internally." Turning to face me with a smile, the nurse said, "Hey, maybe later you can help me give her a bath."

"Really? You can give her bath in her condition?" I asked, pointing to all contraptions around or on her body.

"Yes, it is very good for her circulation. In some cases it helps prevent infections. It's my belief it helps the patient feel better as well. I imagine Jenny would want to be clean."

"Well, then, I'm in. If there's anything I can do to help my wife get better, I'll do it." I was pleased there was something I could do to help Jenny. It made me feel useful.

An hour passed before the nurse came back with a basin of warm water, bath supplies, and a fresh hospital gown for Jenny.

"Are you ready, Alex?"

I was reading a book I had bought at the gift shop earlier that morning. I put it down and said, "Let's get this party started."

Rita and I took turns washing Jenny. We started with Jenny's arms, extra careful not to tug on the many needles sticking into her delicate skin. I supported Jenny's arm as Rita wet it with a white cloth and warm water and washed it with soap. As I poured the warm water over Jenny's bare skin, it responded with goose bumps when the cool air chilled her wet skin. We worked quickly, washing small areas at a time to prevent Jenny from getting chilled.

As we moved to Jenny's legs, I noticed the stubble starting to grow. Knowing Jenny hated having hairy legs, I asked Rita, "Can we shave her legs?"

"It's not a good idea. We risk cutting her skin and creating an open wound. If that happened, it would be likely spot for an infection."

"Oh, okay. It's just that she hates having hairy legs." Not able to do a simple act like shaving Jenny's legs dropped me from the high I had been riding a moment before.

"I understand, but this way it's less likely she'll get an infection. She has enough going on. She doesn't need a razor cut."

"I guess you're right. I know one thing—she's going to need a package of razors to get through the hair when she's well enough to shave them," I said with a laugh.

When we finished bathing Jenny, I thanked Rita for taking such good care of my wife. "Everyone here has been very supportive and caring. I can't thank you guys enough."

"You're welcome. We are all here because we love to help people." Rita says as she gathers her supplies.

"It takes a special type of person to be a nurse." I say smiling at her, thinking Jenny would make a great nurse.

The doctor stopped by Jenny's room after lunch to let me know about Jenny's test results. Dr. Winters was optimistic.

"It would appear there has been a decrease in brain swelling. We compared the test we took yesterday to her first MRI, and the differences are promising. Her heart rate and blood pressure show improvement, and it's been more than twenty-four hours since she last flat-lined. These are all encouraging results. If she keeps up this pattern, it won't be long before you see your wife breathing on her own.

"It's still not clear how the accident affected her brain function and her ability to move her limbs. We will have to wait to see—time will tell. Some of her reflexes are strong; she is responsive to touch on the soles of her feet, but we need to wait for her to improve before checking other responses."

"Thank you, Dr. Winters." I was thankful we were in the best hospital in the state, and I was becoming more hopeful that Jenny would heal. It was just a matter if time. "I feel the hospital has done everything possible to help my wife. Waiting is the hardest part. I just wish there was some drug to give to wake her up." I stood next to Jenny's bed, touching the spot on her forehead that wasn't bandaged. "You should have known her before the accident. She was full of life and greeted every day with deep appreciation for her life and our family. Everyone wanted her energy. She accomplished in a day what would take most people three days. She was focused and determined. Nothing stopped her from getting what she wanted. Nothing."

"Well, Alex, those are very positive attributes. I think she will surprise you. I'm sure she is using that energy to heal herself. If you keep talking to her, she'll fight to get back to the life she once had. I've seen it happen before. A will to live is an attitude; the patient has to want it. If Jenny's love for life is as deep as you just described, I have full faith that she will pull out of this."

"I hope you're right, doctor," I said, shaking his hand. "Thanks."

I was surprised to see Jenny's parents in the doorway.

"Hey, guys! What a surprise! I didn't think you were coming by today, especially so late." It was close to dinnertime.

Jenny's mom spoke first. "Alex, we came by so you could go see Nicolas and Jessica. They have been asking for you, and we think it's time for you to take a break from the hospital. Your mother set up the guest room for you, so you can stay at your parents' house with the kids. It will be good for you and for the kids."

After the great day with Jenny, I picked up Ann's hand. "No, I can't leave her."

Bob interrupted. "Alex, what good will you be if you're overtired and exhausted? You need a break. You've been here for two days. I'll drive you to your parents' house tonight. In the morning after the kids go to school, either your parents or I will bring you back here."

"I know you think that is the right thing, but I belong here. I belong with Jenny. What if she wakes up? I want to be here."

"Think about the children, Alex." Bob and Ann stared at me. "They are missing both of their parents. We can't bring Jenny home, but at least you can go to them."

Ann took my hand and looked me in the eye. "I know it's hard to leave."

I swallowed hard because I was beginning to agree with them.

Ann continued. "I will stay with her all night. She'll never be alone. I will sleep in the chair and make sure she is comfortable. Please, Alex, go see your children."

As I looked down at my wife in the bed, I knew my in-laws were right. It was as if I could hear Jenny speak to me, urging me to go to my parents' for the night. I needed to see Nicolas and Jessica; they needed their father, and it wasn't fair that I was hiding out at the hospital. They deserved to have their father with them, even if only for a night.

Leaning down toward Jenny's ear, I whispered good-bye. "I don't want to leave you, but I think it is important to spend some time with the kids. They are confused, they miss us, and it might help them to see me. I love you, Jenny. I will be back in the morning. Keep resting. I'll see you tomorrow."

Alex

I HAD BEEN HOLED UP IN THE HOSPITAL FOR TWO DAYS WITH THE easy tasks of watching over Jenny, eating in the cafeteria, and finding solace at the hospital chapel. As Bob maneuvered his sedan around the corners of the parking garage and drove to the highway ramp, I noticed my heart rate increase. My breathing was uneven. The engine opened up as we raced down the highway, easily pushing seventy-five miles per hour. I felt every curve and every bump from the uneven pavement, and I was overwhelmed by the stimulation of noise and visual distractions. Bob picked up on my uneasiness.

"Are you okay?" Bob drove in the middle lane. When I looked in the side mirror, I noticed a line of traffic building up behind us. Bob didn't seem fazed by the commuters urging him to go faster.

"I'm not sure how I feel at the moment. But I see there's a world out here away from the one I've been living in the hospital. It's a bit too much for my brain right now."

"You have been living in a bubble at the hospital, surrounded by the constant beeps and swooshes of the machines. There haven't been many changes to your environment. I think your senses are in overdrive."

"I didn't expect life outside of the hospital to affect me like this. I didn't realize that I had stopped living my life when Jenny got in the accident. All my thoughts and attention shifted to Jenny's welfare. I felt I had to make sure she was comfortable and okay. It was enough for me to just eat and brush my teeth." I shook my head with embarrassment; I couldn't remember when I last showered.

The driver of the car behind us finally had an opportunity to pass. When he did, Bob was greeted with an unfriendly gesture that didn't seem to bother him in the least. He accepted it with a nod of his head. I envied the manner in which he held his temper. I, on the other hand, was ready to push Bob out of the car and chase the guy down.

"Alex, it will be good for you to go to your parents' house for a home-cooked meal, a hot shower, and the kids. They are missing you and Jenny so much. I think you'll find them to be therapeutic too."

"Thank you for convincing me to go, Bob. I had my blinders on back at the hospital and didn't see I was starting to fall apart. I feel so powerless there. I can't do anything to help her, but just being with her makes me feel I am doing something for her. It's been hard on me." My eyes shifted as they focused on the white lane markers in the road.

"Jenny is very lucky to have a husband like you, Alex. Ann and I will be forever grateful to you for the way that you have stayed by her side through this."

"She's a special girl, but you already know that." I caught myself smiling, knowing Jenny's the ultimate Daddy's girl. Bob had spoiled her all her life, and I picked up where he left off.

Relief set in when I saw the exit for my parents' house. Getting away from the traffic would help soothe the stimulation overload that bombarded me on the drive from the hospital. I couldn't wait for the drive to end, to be at my parents' house.

As I walked through the front door, I heard dinner plates and utensils clanging, and the smell of dinner made my mouth water. No one heard the door open, and they didn't know I was in the house until they saw me walk into the kitchen.

"Daddy!" Both kids ran to me and almost knocked me over. "We missed you. Is Mom with you?"

"Sorry, guys. The doctors wouldn't let her come with me this time." I tousled Nicolas's hair with my hand. "Maybe next time. But, she is getting stronger. The doctors are really happy with her progress."

I sat down at the table to eat, Nicolas on one side and Jessica on the other. My mother's home-cooked meal was the remedy I needed after eating cafeteria-grade food for two days. After filling myself up with the roast beef dinner, I suddenly felt the impact of the last two days. By stepping away from my constant concentration on Jenny, I was able to feel how tired I had become, and now I was thankful to be at my parents' house, taking a break from the hospital.

After dinner I played card games with kids and we talked about school. Nicolas told me about the art project he had completed yesterday. His teacher taught the class about watercolor paintings, and he'd brought his home. He was excited to show it to me. When I saw it, I thought it was a masterpiece. He'd painted a scene of a pond with little fish swimming and colorful birds flying in the sky. He painted the sun in the left corner, and a little person holding a fishing rod sat on a rock near the water's edge. I was surprised by all the details Nicolas put into the painting.

"Nicolas, you are quite the artist. What are you planning on doing with this?"

"Mom usually puts our art work in a folder in the playroom closet at home."

Staring at the painting, I had a better idea. I turned to look at Nicolas. "Hey, buddy. Do you think I could bring it to show Mom at the hospital? I bet she would love to see it."

"Yeah, Dad, that would be great." I could see the pride shining in his eyes.

After I put the kids to bed and went downstairs, I found my parents sitting in the family room. I had to laugh. My father sat in his big Daddy chair, watching the updates on the sporting events, while my mother sat in her chair, knitting.

"You guys haven't changed a bit."

"Hi, honey. Are the kids in bed? Can I get you anything?" My mother stood as I walked into the room.

"No thanks, Mom. I'm good. I read them a couple of books and tucked them in tight, so they should be asleep in no time." I plunked down on the couch in the middle of the room between my parents and put my feet on the coffee table. "I thought I would hang out with you before heading to bed. Although my bed might be right here — I might not be able to get up again." I was crashing in the aftermath of the surges of adrenaline that had kept me alert at the hospital.

"How about the Red Sox slaughtering the Angels?" My dad had NESN on; the city was still celebrating and buzzing about the wins.

"Yeah, I saw the headlines all over the newspapers in the gift shop. I have been so consumed with taking care of Jenny I forgot all about the series. I didn't even think to watch the games." It was one of many things I had let go of and lost interest in since Jenny's accident. Her health was the most important thing in my life at the moment.

We spent the next hour talking and catching up on current events and family news. I could tell they were hesitant about bringing up Jenny's condition, and they danced around the subject, so I started the conversation.

"The doctor came by Jenny's room earlier today and told me she is making some progress."

"I wanted to ask you how she was doing, but didn't want to upset you. I thought you might like to avoid talking about it for the night, but I'm glad to hear that. What else did he say?" my mother asked, moving her knitting needles in rhythm to create a woven pattern with the cream-colored yarn. She had been knitting for so many years, she was able to carry on full conversations without looking at her yarn, and she never missed a stitch. She joked she could knit blindfolded.

"The swelling has come down some, and her reflexes are good. There's no way to tell if there is permanent damage from the accident or when she'll wake up. We have to wait to see if she will have any mobility." My voice changed and became heavier. I began to feel nauseated, thinking about the future and what it could be like for Jenny and me.

My father was aware of the sudden shift in my emotions. "She's a tough girl, Alex. She'll surprise you, son," my dad said. He loved Jenny like a daughter.

"I hope so, Dad."

I ran the shower to warm up the water, and while I waited I looked at my reflection in the mirror above the sink. I didn't recognize the man in front of me. Sure, it was me—I knew that—but the image I saw was of a tired old man, a man who had been put through too much too quickly—a worn-out man who needed a break, a chance to breathe, to organize the thoughts and emotions that had been challenged by something out of his control. I'd needed someone to call me to the bench and rebuild me, to refocus my attention and set me straight, like a good coach would call a timeout during the final minutes of a tied game. Steam began to fill the room and fogged the mirror. I placed my hand under the spray of hot water falling from the shower head. My timeout began.

I stood in the shower, feeling the warm water race over the surfaces of my body. My skin was enjoying the therapeutic massage from the pulsating water jets, and I felt my muscles release and stretch as I moved the washcloth over my skin. Feeling a new sense of calm, I scrubbed the oils from my hair and rinsed the shampoo out. As the water ran down my back, washing away the stress I had built up over the past two days, I felt a deeper sense of relaxation. I didn't want my timeout to end. I enjoyed the peace and comfort I found in the sound and warmth of the water. I needed to pack a travel bag for the hospital, so I could steal timeouts in the shower there too.

Like a new man, refreshed, I climbed between the sheets of a real bed. Any leftover aches after the rejuvenating shower were released as the mattress cradled my body and supported my weight. I laid my head on the pillow and felt my muscles relax from my head down throughout my body, muscle by muscle, an unwrapping of emotions. It felt good to be supported and to shed my stress.

As I laid there, the moonlight sneaking in from the sides of the window shades, I noticed the silence in the room, and I thought of Jenny lying in the hospital bed in a room with noisy machines robbing her of silence. I started to pray for Jenny's recovery, for strength, and for our families.

I'm not sure I finished my conversation with God; my last memory was of beginning my prayer. The next thing I knew I had two bodies next to me, Nicolas on one side and Jessica on the other.

"Good morning, Dad."

"Hi, Daddy."

"Good morning, guys. How long have you been here?" My voice sounded as groggy as I felt. I cracked open my eyes and saw light breaking through the sides of the curtains; a new day was starting.

"Just a few minutes. We wanted to wake you up sooner, but Mimi wouldn't let us. Breakfast is ready." Jessica was sticking her fingers in my eyes, trying to pry them open.

"I can smell it. I'll be right down." Lifting her hand away from my eyes, I kissed it and started tickling her.

"Get him, Nicolas! Help me!" Each word emerged between a breath. Jessica was very ticklish, just like her mother.

I left myself exposed to Nicolas's attack on my neck, right where it attached to the collarbone. He got me good. I released Jessica to stop him, and she took the opportunity to jump on top of me. I tried to grab Nicolas's arms and missed, and Jessica went on jumping on top of me. They had me beat.

I yelled out, "Mercy!" I was too tired to wrestle. I needed to reserve the energy I had to get through the day at the hospital. "Mercy!"

That thrilled them, and they ran out of the room yelling, "We beat Daddy. We beat Daddy!"

I rolled over, not ready to meet the day ahead. I could have slept for another ten hours, easily.

I sat at the kitchen table, pleased to be sharing breakfast with my kids rather than eating hospital food alone in the cafeteria. I appreciated their company while I enjoyed my mother's scrambled egg break-fast with toast and a fresh cup of coffee. I felt comfortable being in a home, not a hospital.

Nicolas and Jessica were excited when I told them I would drive them to school, but didn't understand why I had to go back to the hospital later and not see them for a couple more days.

"Mommy stills needs me to be with her at the hospital, and I need to be there to talk to the doctors and take care of Mommy. I'm sorry this is happening to us, guys, but you get to stay here. Mimi will take good care of you." I hugged and kissed them. When I pulled back, I could see the hurt in their eyes, and it stung me.

"Oh, guys, I know it hurts. Come here." I held them both in my arms, wishing I could protect them from all this, but I knew I had no control over the situation. It was out of my hands.

I looked into their eyes and made a promise to them that this would be over soon and we would be back home as a family. I didn't know what the family dynamic would look like, but all the kids needed to hear was that we would all be together again. I believed it would happen. I just didn't know what condition Jenny would be in.

Sitting behind the steering wheel of my mother's car as I drove the kids to school, I felt like I hadn't driven in months. Pulling up to the curb, I told them I would see them soon. As they stepped out of the car, they saw their friends coming off the bus. Any sour emotions from the kitchen table dissolved as they ran off to catch up to their friends, yelling, "Bye, Dad."

"Have a great day, guys." The door slammed shut before the words were completely out of my mouth. I envied the ease with which a child's emotions could shift depending on the stimulus around them. Having the structure of school and good friends helped them to put their mother's tenuous condition aside for the moment. They knew it would be there later to deal with, but for now there was fun waiting to be had on the playground. I sat in the car and smiled as Nicolas and

Jessica caught up with their friends. The bright smiles I saw on their faces reminded me that life goes on.

I drove into my parents' driveway and noticed Bob sitting in his car under the maple tree. I drove into the garage as Bob got out of his car and waited in the driveway.

"Ready?"

"Let me say good-bye to my parents. I'll be right out."

I grabbed the bag I had packed at home after dropping the kids at school and got into Bob's car. I was torn about leaving the peace of my parents' house and going back to the stress of the hospital, but at least I would be with Jenny.

"Did you speak to Ann this morning? Are there any changes with Jenny?"

"Yes, we spoke briefly when she woke up, but there was nothing new to report."

Looking out the car window as we approached the highway, I said, "Well, I suppose that's better than bad news."

Most of the commuter traffic had thinned out, and only a few tangles of congestion remained. The farther we drove, the more anxious I became as I thought about getting to the hospital. Another part of my life was continuing there without me. It seemed to be taking a long time to get there; Bob wasn't driving fast enough for me.

When we pulled into the parking garage, I was relieved to be back at the hospital with Jenny. It had become familiar to me, and I had developed a routine in the three days since Jenny's accident. The hospital had once been a maze to me. I would walk down corridors and every hall looked the same, but now I could tell which floor I was on and the department I was walking through. I found shortcuts and stairways that were faster than the elevators, and I knew the slow ones from the fast ones. But from the parking garage, there was only one way to Jenny's room, and it felt like it was miles away. Like a little kid on Christmas morning, I wanted to run to my presents, see them and touch them. My present was Jenny. I wanted to run to her, to see and touch her again.

When I finally reached her room, I was immediately comforted by her presence. Bob was right, nothing had changed; everything looked just like it had when I left yesterday. But I had changed after a good night's sleep. I had more energy, and I knew that would help me bring better energy to Jenny.

Looking around the boring white hospital room, I found a place away from the machines and Jenny's IV pole to hang Nicolas's artwork. I hung it on the cabinet door above the sink, just to the left of the doorway. I wanted it be the first thing she saw when she opened her eyes.

The painting offered a relaxing place to rest one's eyes, to appreciate the colors and details that added a cheerful touch to the otherwise boring room. I decided there should be more artwork in hospital rooms, not only for the patients to enjoy while they healed, but also to give visitors something to look at besides their bedridden family member and the CPR diagrams.

I couldn't help but notice the puffy, dark rings around Ann's eyes as she filled me in about the night. It didn't look like she'd gotten much sleep. She mentioned that Jenny's brother, Paul, was returning from vacation and would stop by the hospital later in the day.

"He's going to have a hard time seeing his baby sister like this." She was holding back tears; her eyes were full of emotion. "He always wanted to protect her. He would ride his bike behind hers, just in case she fell, so he could get to her quickly. That's the kind of big brother he was. They were very close growing up, but somehow life goes on and people grow apart. He was devastated when I told him about the accident. He wanted to be here, but I told him there was nothing he could do, and he should enjoy the rest of his vacation. Jenny would have wanted it that way."

"Ann, Jenny has always spoken lovingly of Paul. I know they have a special place in their hearts for each other. Life gets harder as we grow and have more responsibilities, but I bet they know how much they love each other. I'll make sure I'm here when Paul comes by. Don't worry." I rubbed her arm.

"Alex, you're a good man. I am glad Jenny found you and you guys made it work." She barely got the words out before a yawn took over.

"Thanks, Ann. Me too." I looked at Jenny and said a silent prayer that she would come back to me soon.

Ann and Bob soon left to go home and rest.

Just before dinner, Paul came around the corner to Jenny's room and stopped in the doorway.

"Oh my God. It can't be this bad. Look at her!" He put his hand over his mouth, frozen in the doorway.

I walked over to him. "Paul, come in. It's good to see you." I hugged him to greet him and also to keep him from falling over. I tried to explain the situation to him. "At first sight it seems very overwhelming, but once you're here for a while and see what is happening, you can make better sense of it."

"Oh, man. I can't believe this. I can't believe this happened to her." I recognized the shock on his face and knew I must have looked the same for the first day or two.

"I'm glad you're here, Paul. I bet if you talk to her, she'll know you're here. She squeezed my mom's hand when she was talking to her, and she tried to squeeze mine, but it wasn't as strong."

"She did?" Standing feet away from Jenny, his gaze never left his baby sister, who lay in a hospital bed fighting for her life. "What is the prognosis? Will she regain consciousness? Will she walk and talk? How long will she be like this?"

"We don't know all the answers yet. It's a waiting game at this point. She is showing signs of improvement, but it may be days or weeks before we know more. She's a fighter, though, Paul—you know that." I went to Jenny and picked up her hand to kiss it.

Paul walked over to the bedside. "Can I hold her hand?"

"Yeah, sure. Why don't I let you have some alone time with her. I'll go grab some dinner and be back in about forty-five minutes. Is that all right?"

"Yeah, I would appreciate that."

Jenny

"JENNY, I CAN'T BELIEVE THIS HAPPENED TO YOU. I DIDN'T THINK IT would be this bad. I'm kind of in shock. You have got to wake up — if anyone can do it, you can. Come on, Sis. We all need you. Christ, Jenny, your kids need you." Tears fell from Paul's eyes as he sat by my bed, pleading for me to wake up. If only he knew how hard I was trying and that I was able to hear everything he said.

Wiping his tears away, Paul began recalling many childhood memories and the crazy things we did. He retold his favorite one about the time our dad was napping in his chair on a weekend afternoon, a time when our dad often nodded off. We snuck up on him, put whipped cream in his palm, and tickled his nose with a feather. When he felt the feather touch his nose, he brushed it away with a palm full of whipped cream. We laughed hard at the sight of our dad in his chair with whipped cream all over his face. But when he woke up he was by no means amused. We apologized and ran outside to play and hide from him.

Paul and I were very close as kids and still had a great relationship. From the look on his face, I could see that he was scared. It was clear that seeing me in this condition broke his heart. I loved him, and I didn't want to be the cause of his sadness. It hurt me to see him like that. For many years he tried to protect me, and I tried to protect him from seeing me get hurt, but now I couldn't do anything about it, and neither could he.

Paul was older than me by three years. Whenever I went out, either with my friends or alone, he worried about me. I always wondered if our mother made him that way. Paul was there when I needed him, and he cared about me down to the depths of his being. When I had my first broken heart in eighth grade, he was there to help me mend, and when I didn't make the church choir, he took me for an ice cream to put a smile on my face. I loved him very much. Now I realized how much I had missed having him as a part of my adult life. There were no excuses for not continuing and honoring our relationship. I decided when I woke up from this accident, I was going to appreciate life on a much different level. I would be getting a second chance.

I was so absorbed in watching Paul grieve for me, I was startled when Alex came in the room after dinner. I watched and listened to the conversation between the two men I cared for.

"Man, I'm so sorry you have to be going through this." Paul got up and hugged Alex.

"You know your sister—she was probably looking for attention," Alex joked. I didn't appreciate that comment, but he knows I would do just about anything for attention. It must have to do with being the youngest.

"She didn't have to go to this extent to get it," Paul said.

Alex placed his hand on Paul's shoulder and said, "Ya know, I think she'll be okay. A lot of people are praying for her, and she got medical attention quickly. She is in a great hospital with great doctors. All we can do is pray and wait."

I saw Paul look over at Alex with a perplexed look. "That doesn't sound right coming from you. You and praying, in the same sentence? Has she changed you that much?"

"This whole experience has changed me, Paul."

"She'd be proud of you," Paul said with a sincere smile and a nod. He turned and put his jacket on.

"It was good to see you, man. Come by whenever you want. I'll be here," Alex told him.

"Thanks for taking care of her. We all appreciate it. Take care of yourself too." Paul left the room.

I floated above, a smile on my face. I was proud of my husband — and amazed. Alex was praying? I was filled with new emotions, admiring Alex for giving in and letting prayer carry him. I realized he would never be the same man I knew before the accident. When I got well, I would be married to a more accepting man who loved more deeply. I couldn't wait.

I was also proud of my family's loving ways. Everyone was so supportive of one another, and the way they loved and cared about me showed me how blessed I was.

Alex shared stories with me that night about the kids. I loved seeing the smile on his face when he talked about them. He was a great dad and a great husband. I decided Alex was the greatest person to ever live. I was happy to have him by my side, and when I woke up, I would tell him so.

Alex

"HI, HONEY. IT FEELS GOOD TO BE BACK WITH YOU TONIGHT AND to be alone again." I caressed Jenny's shoulder. "I miss you, Jenny. I miss talking to you. I miss your smile and your laugh." I touched her cheek with the back of my hand. "Jenny, I know you're in there, and I believe you can hear me. I love you so much. I've never stopped. Please wake up and come back to us. Everyone wants you to wake up." I stared at her face, the face of the girl who changed my life with just one glance. She still held the power to bring me to my knees. Jenny was my better half. We were best friends and partners in crime. In my mind, no one loved as deeply as we did. I knew I couldn't live without her.

"I went to see the kids last night. They look great. They asked about you, of course, and I told them you had a headache and the doctors were taking very good care of you. I explained you'll come home as soon as your headache goes away. I think they understood me." I took hold of her hand. "My parents love having them around. I hope they don't get used to it! Nicolas painted that picture over there near the door. I can't wait for you to see it. He is very talented. Maybe we should get him into an art class? He was so proud of himself. Jessica is as cute as ever. We had a fun night playing checkers — she beat me. She's coming along with her piano lessons too. She played a song for me, and it sounded great. I should record her next time and have you listen to it." *I'll do that*, I thought to myself.

As I got my makeshift bed ready, the nurse came by to check on Jenny.

"Everything looks good. Are you staying tonight?"

"Yes, I'll be here."

"We'll try not to disturb you unless something comes up. Good night. See you in the morning."

Alex

JENNY'S PROGRESS WAS SLOW, BUT THE CT SCANS AND MRIS showed some improvement. The doctors were happy with what they saw, but I would be happier when I could hear my wife's voice. Every day brought new hope that she would wake up. When the day ended it carried the hope away with it.

The week following the accident I stayed at the hospital most of the time, but on Saturday morning Ann and Bob arrived to stay with Jenny, so that I could leave for the day. I planned to spend the day watching Nicolas and Jessica play soccer and then have dinner with them before returning.

I returned to the hospital, and Jenny's parents left for the evening, I sat next to Jenny. "Hi, Jenny, I'm back. The kids did great at their soccer games. Nicolas had two goals and Jessica got one — they were very excited. I brought them to their favorite restaurant, Creek's, for dinner. Don't worry, I made sure they ate their veggies. They send their love and really miss you. I told them I would tell you how much they miss you and want you to come back home." I kissed the exposed area on her forehead. "Jenny, tomorrow is Sunday. It's been one week since you've been here. Please, honey, please wake up. Your tests are looking good, your blood pressure and oxygen saturation levels are great, your heart rate is strong, and your body temperature is normal. We're just waiting for you to open those beautiful eyes.

"Jenny, I have to tell you something. I've been praying. I know it's a shocker — you should have seen your brother's face. It's been interesting. At first I felt weird, like I was talking to myself. But when I was finished, I felt lighter. I sat for a while, just feeling the change. I've been to the chapel in the hospital. It's beautiful, and I think you would enjoy it. The peace it brings is refreshing. I think it has helped me carry on this past week. I am putting my faith in God. I think—no, I know—that in all the years when I tried to control my life, it would have been easier to put it in God's hands and understand I can only do so much. There is a magic to life I never saw before. Honey, you always tried to make me see it, but I think it took this, for me see. Otherwise, I would still think I was my own master. I hate that it had to come to me this way. Jenny, my love, I believe and have a faith in God deeper than I ever thought I would. Faith is all I have now. I can't make you wake up— it's in his hands." I pointed up to Heaven.

"I can't do anything but talk to you and pray. Every day I visit the chapel and say a prayer for you and me and the kids. It warms my soul to be able to go someplace and talk where no one can judge me. I just sit and talk, and when I'm done, I feel alive. You tried for years to bring me to church and encouraged me to pray when life was challenging, but I always resisted. Now I want to thank you for teaching me the power in praying." I held her hand and continued. "It's night time, time for me to try to sleep. Tomorrow is Sunday. Maybe that will be the day I can see your sparkling eyes and hear your voice. I can only hope and pray. I love you. Sweet dreams."

The morning came fast. Before I knew it, the sun's rays were shining in the room. I slept well enough through the noises of the hospital; I had become numb to, and thankful for, the sounds of the machines that kept Jenny alive. I got out of bed and looked out of the window as the sun lit up the world and the trees swayed gently in the breeze. When I looked at the tree limb just outside Jenny's window, I had to blink and focus. A dove was perched outside Jenny's window. When I looked closer, I noticed the partner dove sitting a few branches below. A smile came over my face, and I wondered if it could be a sign. I went to Jenny and held her hand. "Honey, I just saw two doves outside your window. I think they came to tell me you're going to be okay." I kissed her forehead and left to get breakfast.

I returned after breakfast and praying at the chapel. The sound in the room was different—it was quieter because the noise from the ventilator was gone. Jenny was still attached to the IV line and the blood pressure machine, but not the ventilator. An oxygen mask now replaced her breathing tube, and it appeared she was breathing on her own. No one had prepared me for this. I had to find the nurse.

"What is going on? Why is she off the ventilator? What the hell is happening?" Rapid-fire, I questioned the nurse at the nurse's station.

"The doctor went by the room to see you, but you had already left. He made a decision based on her latest results to test her independent breathing, and he removed her from the ventilator."

I stood in shock. "Is it safe?"

"It's been a week since she came in, and all her bodily functions are normal. We can't keep her hooked up to the ventilator forever. She needs to start to breathe on her own."

As the nurse was explaining, Dr. Winters walked over and shook my hand. "Alex, good morning. I came to see you earlier but you weren't in the room."

Trying to keep my patience and not sound too harsh, I asked the doctor, "What is going on?"

"I can tell you've seen your wife. I think it is best if we go to the family room, where we can talk in private."

We sat at the small table in the corner of the family room. I looked around. The furniture was arranged to mimic a family living room, but the feeling was much different. I imagined the different scenarios that had and would play out in this room I pictured a doctor flipping a coin—heads, you live; tails, you die. The room gave me the creeps. I was happier in the hallway.

"We made the decision to remove your wife from the ventilator. She is showing signs of improving. If we keep her on the ventilator any longer, it may cause further damage. Her blood pressure and heart rate are stronger, better than when she came in, in the normal range now, and her body is beginning to heal. Look—these are Jenny's CT scan and MRI from last Sunday; these are from Wednesday, and these are from yesterday. You can see for yourself that the bleeding and swelling are diminishing and the head trauma is returning to normal." He used his pen to point out the shaded gray areas and the improvements over the last week.

"I spoke with the team of doctors involved in Jenny's care, and we all agreed with this decision. We will see what the day brings, but I am hopeful she will continue to breathe on her own. The oxygen mask will help her body get the proper amount of oxygen from breathing independently." Taking his glasses off and looking me in the eyes, he continued. "Alex, these are all good signs. I understand it is hard to see things change, but please know we are doing what is best for your wife. She is strong, and we are reacting to what her body is telling us. She is ready for this step."

I was speechless, having a hard time wrapping my head around everything the doctor just told me. Dr. Winters was right—I wasn't ready. I had become used to the machines breathing for her. I had carried a false belief that attached to the machines, there was no way Jenny could die. I believed she would live because they did the work for her. But now she was on her own. I sat quietly for a minute, thinking. I didn't want to ask the question that was banging around in my head, but I knew I had to. "Doctor, what happens if she stops breathing?"

"We don't believe that's likely, but if it were to happen we would put her back on the ventilator. Alex, from what her body has shown us over the last few days, she is ready. There haven't been any incidents of respiratory failure since early last week, and we believe she is progressing. Her medical history from the last week shows us she's ready."

"You sound very convincing. I hope you're right." I stood. "I do trust you. I just wasn't prepared for her to be off the machine." Shaking his hand, I said, "Thank you. I want to go to my wife now."

"Yes, by all means. I will come with you."

The room had a different feel to it, quieter without the profound noise of the ventilator that used to drown out the silence. Being there without the machine made me feel raw and alone. I'd grown attached to the noises that kept Jenny alive. Without them, I was anxious that her lifeline was cut off. In time, I was sure that I would become grateful for the oxygen mask's softer sound, a peaceful hush rather than the unnerving rhythmic noise of the ventilator. I could relax to the consistent hushed flow of oxygen.

Dr. Winters walked over to Jenny. "Alex, look here. Her wounds and abrasions are looking better." He moved his fingers over some of the cuts Jenny had suffered from being knocked around in the car. "The nurse removed Jenny's bandages this morning, and when she saw how well they were healing, we decided to remove most of them. Some will stay on, like this bandage here," pointing to Jenny's forearm, "because the cut was deeper. It hasn't healed as well as the others."

I could see more of Jenny's skin now. Her bruises from the dashboard and steering wheel were purple. The scrapes and cuts were starting to scab over. Soon enough they would all be healed and this would be just be a memory.

"So we continue to wait. How do we know when she will wake up?" I looked up at Dr. Winter, waiting for the answer to the million-dollar question.

"I think we will see more signs of improvement this week. I can't say for sure when she will wake up, but I believe she will." Dr. Winters walked to the door. "I need to check on my other patients. I will come back to check on her again before I leave for the day. Alex, please remember she was ready for this. Keep encouraging her. She can hear you."

"Thanks, doctor."

I pulled my chair closer to Jenny's bed and began stroking her skin. With most of the bandages removed, I could now touch her in places I hadn't been able to. Her skin was dry, lacking moisture to nourish it. I fumbled around on the nightstand and found the lotion Rita and I had used after we last bathed her. As I rubbed it into her skin, it reminded me of all the times Jenny had begged me to massage her back and legs. I watched her skin drink in the moisture, as if I could hear her speaking, "Alex, I've had a long day, and I'm tired from chasing the kids. Can you please rub my back? Oh, while you're at it, don't forget my legs and feet." She always wore a sweet, innocent expression on her face that made it impossible to resist her. What I wouldn't give today to hear her voice asking me for a massage. I would be glad to do it and would get more satisfaction from it than she would.

Seeing her lying in bed with less hospital gear to help her stay alive made me think of the progress she'd made. It was a good day. If the team of doctors on Jenny's case believed in her body's ability to take the next step and breathe on its own, I wanted to believe too. So I sat and watched her lungs take in air and move it out—not big breaths, but she was doing it on her own. Seeing was believing.

When Ann and Bob walked into the room later, they were as shocked as I had been. Without the background noise from the ventilator, I didn't have to strain to hear the confusion in Bob's voice.

"What happened?" he asked.

"Hi, Ann. Hi, Bob." I stood up to greet my in-laws. "The doctors said she is ready for this step, so they took her off the ventilator this morning. A shocker, right? I left to get breakfast and stopped at the chapel. When I came back this is how I found her. I guess it's good news. She's making progress."

"Well, it's certainly a shock. And a lot quieter," Ann remarked. "It's nice to see her hooked up to less machinery and without so many bandages. She's been through so much." Ann held Jenny's hand, her face worried as she stared at her daughter lying still in the hospital bed.

The tension was growing, and I had to cut it fast. Walking to the window, I looked for signs that the doves had returned. I told Ann and

Bob, "You guys won't believe what I saw this morning. Two doves were sitting in the tree outside this window. I think it's a sign."

Ann's attention shifted, "Oh, Alex, I think it's a great sign. We should continue to have faith Jenny will be okay. Alex, word is spreading about Jenny's condition. We just came from church, and everyone is praying for Jenny and for you and the children. The community has been putting out information about Jenny's progress. There's talk about having a charity drive to help cover some of the hospital bills. I think the school PTO is behind it all. The members and the school have been wonderful with the kids. Your mother was telling me she's been receiving meals at her house from Nicolas and Jessica's classmate's families. Can you believe that?"

I was speechless. I had shut myself off from the outside world since Jenny's accident, so there was no way of knowing people were helping us from the behind the scenes. It never dawned on me that people would make meals for my family, but I was grateful that we lived in a community that reached out to help families.

"I guess it speaks to how much people love Jenny and how much she has done to help others. Treat others as you want to be treated, right? That's what Jenny always said." Ann turned to Jenny, a tearing running down her cheek. "If only she could see how true those words are."

We sat together all afternoon, waiting for Jenny to open her eyes or move her hand — anything to show us she would be all right. We took turns eating lunch and never left her alone. Someone had to be there if she spoke or opened her eyes.

As the day passed into night, no changes came. Ann and Bob were getting ready to leave.

"I think we'll come back tomorrow. I don't think Jenny should be alone for a second. Someone should always be by her side," Ann said. "And you shouldn't have to be here by yourself all the time. Even a big, strong man like you deserves a break." She smiled at me.

"Thanks, Ann. I enjoy your company."

"I will call your mother later and update her. She has been trying to get here, but she's been very busy lately taking care of your children," Ann said, teasing me.

"Thanks, I appreciate it." I hugged my mother-in-law and shook my father-in-law's hand. "I'll see you guys in the morning."

The next morning I was woken up by the nurse. "Hi. Good morning! Sorry to wake you, but I need to check on the patient. She had a good night. When I came by to check on her, you were sound asleep. It's good to get your rest because she's going to need you when she wakes up." She smiled at me as she busied herself around Jenny's bed, checking the oxygen levels and turning Jenny to her other side.

I got up to help her and asked, "You think she is going to be okay?"

"Well, we will have to wait for her to regain full consciousness to understand how much like her old self she will be. These types of injuries can have many mental impacts on a patient. But I think there are a lot of promising signs. For instance, her tests are looking better, and she's breathing on her own without the ventilator. She is a fighter, this one, and I think God is on her side."

Looking down at my wife, I knew the nurse was right. Jenny was a fighter and very faithful. Maybe that combination had carried her through this. I knew one thing for myself; faith was all I had now.

After Jenny's parents left that afternoon, my parents came to see Jenny. Ann and Bob were taking care of Nicolas and Jessica for the night to give my parents a break.

My parents arrived at the hospital carrying a bag of clothes for me plus a music player and Jenny's favorite CDs. "Thanks for bringing this for me, Mom. I could use a change of clothes." I saw she had found all the CDs I asked for. "I don't know why it took me so long to think of playing music for her. If Jenny can hear us talk to her, then she'll be able to hear music. We should play her favorite music to help her get better. It will also break the silence and change the mood."

"It's a great idea, Alex," my mom assured me. She gave me a big hug and kiss. "How are you doing? I don't want to hear 'fine, okay, hanging in there'. I really want to know—how are you?"

As I started to fiddle with the buttons on the music player, I could tell my dad picked up on my uneasiness. He suggested he would get some coffee and come back in a bit. I appreciated the privacy as he left the room.

"Mom, thanks for asking. I don't really have anyone to talk to. Jenny has always been the one I turn to. I do talk to her now, but obviously it's not the same." My eyes must have revealed the pain I felt inside, the pain I had been concealing as I tried to be strong for everyone. After a week of fighting between hope and despair, my pillars were beginning to crack.

My mother simply said, "Talk to me."

"I just don't know how we got here and why this is happening to her, to us." I paced around the room as I talked. "Ya know, one minute you're living your life, going about your business, and then boom, it's all flipped upside down. I have been having a hard time getting my mind around it." I stopped and looked at my mother. "Okay, this is what I mean. I get she's in the hospital and we're waiting for her to wake up, but when she does, what then? We don't even know what she's going to be like. We don't know if she has suffered serious brain damage." I raked my hands through my greasy hair. "I hate feeling this way and thinking about the 'what if' scenarios, so I tell myself I have to believe she's going to make it and be her normal self again. It's all I have right now. I am determined to see it that way." My mother didn't take her eyes off me, and I continued to vent. "Before this happened, you know I wasn't a believer in prayer or a higher power. But in the darkest times I spent here at the hospital, I went to the chapel to think, and something began to change inside of me. Because of the magnitude of Jenny's condition and the obvious facts that I had no control over what had happened and I couldn't fix it, I turned to God. You and Jenny have always been committed to praying when things were right in your lives and when things turned sour. It's because of you two that I tried praying, seeing there was nothing else I could do."

"Alex, I'm so proud of you. I remember when you told me how you felt after you prayed. You need to keep going back to that feeling. Jenny's situation is not something you can control or could have prevented. Honey, you can and should believe that she will be herself again, but you can't put the responsibility on your shoulders. It just doesn't work that way. In the end, you'll do more damage to yourself than good. I think you should continue to pray, to keep faith she will wake up, and let the rest fall into God's hands. What will be will be." My mother stood at my side and took hold of my hand. "We will discover the severity of Jenny's injuries when she wakes up. Until then, Alex, you can always turn to me. I am here to listen, and I won't judge you. I will guide you. I love you very much, and I think you are handling all of this very well." We turned to embrace.

"Thanks, Mom, I love you too."

Needing to shake off the weight of our conversation, after a moment of silence I said, "Let's get some music playing."

We started with Jenny's childhood favorite "Bad, Bad Leroy Brown." Her grandfather always played it when she was younger, and after he died she often sang it and remembered how much she loved and missed her grandfather.

Jenny

As music filled the room, I moved to the rhythm, the words flooding my ears: "Cuz he was bad, bad Leroy Brown, baddest man in the whole damn town. Badder than ol' King Kong, meaner than a junkyard dog."

I turned to the aura. *Someone's coming.* And in a couple of minutes my grandfather was by my side. "Papa! Oh my, you're here! I can see you."

"Hi, Doll. I hear they're playing our song." There was a glint of happiness and peace in his eye. He held my hand. "Jenny, you don't belong here. Sweetie, you need to fight to wake up. Your family needs you back home."

"I know, Papa, but I can't wake up. Every time I try, it makes me more tired." I turned to look at him. "I've missed you so much, and so has Mom. Do you think I will remember any of this?" I was too excited, and I rambled on. "I've seen my grandchildren, Papa. What a gift I was given! I know I will live. I will wake up. I don't know how I will feel or what my life will be like while I continue to heal."

"Dear, no one knows the future, but we carry on. We need to live in the present moment. It's a gift to be able to live that way. Soon enough you will return to your family. Whatever the outcome is and however you are physically, that doesn't matter. They all love you for being Jenny, not what you can do or how you move." He held me and said, "I love you, Jenny—never forget that. We are all praying for you."

I felt safe in his arms, just like when I was little. I turned to look down at Alex and his mom, reenergized, full of love and strength after seeing my Papa. I had no doubt I would return to Alex and our family. When I turned back to tell my Papa I loved him too, he was gone. I smiled, knowing I would see him again, when it was my time.

I never thought I would see my grandfather again after he lost his battle to cancer. But seeing him now and feeling his love proved I needed to fight to wake up. My family needed to see me again and feel my love, and I needed to feel theirs.

Alex

As the days passed, some changes appeared in Jenny. She was able to squeeze my hand more often. On Thursday, as I filled her in on the children's lives and activities, she fluttered her eyelids. A jolt of electricity went through me. I jumped up to get a nurse. "Come here. She opened her eyes."

The veteran nurse explained that sometimes coma patients displayed uncontrolled reflexes. "It's not a sign she's waking up, any more than her breathing is a sign she's going to have full control over her body."

I was crushed by what the nurse said. "I can believe that's it. I can hope she is waking up." I looked at the stubborn old nurse, full of contempt.

"I understand it's hard. Most families have a difficult time understanding how the body responds to brain injury and trauma. These are involuntary responses. I'm sorry it's not what you were thinking. Also, you should not be alarmed if you hear her mumble or make strange noises; it's all part of the body's reaction to being unconscious."

"Oh, thanks for letting me know. No one told me that." I tried to understand that she meant no harm and had become hardened from exposure to patients similar to Jenny.

The nurse left. I sat in the chair next to Jenny and whispered in her ear. "Jenny, I know you can hear me. I saw you open and close your eyes. I believe you're fighting to come back to me. I'm here. I'm not leaving until I take you home with me. I love you."

Listening to a Madonna song on the music player, I sat back and waited. I watched as her chest rose and fell, and I waited to see her open eyes again, but she never opened them again that day.

On Saturday, Bob and Ann were by Jenny's side when she tried to speak. They heard her utter a sound, but they couldn't make out what Jenny said; it was all garbled. Jenny's parents told me what happened when I returned from lunch.

Bob was at the bedside, frustration in his voice. "We heard Jenny make a noise, but I couldn't understand her, so I asked Ann, 'What did she say?' Ann couldn't make out the words either."

"I don't know what she said. I couldn't understand it, but she tried to speak." Ann's voice trembled. "Oh, I hope she can speak when she wakes up. I hope she isn't paralyzed, unable to live as she lived before."

I recognized that Ann was distraught over the lack of control in Jenny's voice.

Bob stood next to Jenny. "Let's not go there, Ann. We need to stay positive. It's been almost two weeks, and she has come far in those weeks. She will be okay," Bob said, touching his daughter's shoulder. I wasn't sure if he was saying it for his benefit or to calm his wife.

I stood between my in-laws, listening to them. "I shouldn't have left. I need to be here." I was mad I wasn't there when Jenny tried to talk. I didn't want to hear their opinions about Jenny's lack of control over her voice. If I had been there, I would have understood what she said.

"Alex you can't always be here. You need to eat. She'll talk again. Bob's right. She is making strides. We have to keep believing in her. Don't let our frustrations get in the way of Jenny's progress." Ann patted my back.

"You're probably right. I know I can't be here all the time, but I still don't want to miss anything that happens to her." I knew I had to eat and talk to the kids. But in fact, all I really wanted was to stay with Jenny and see my wife open her eyes and hear her talk to me again.

When I woke up Sunday morning, my stomach reminded me it had been too long since my last meal. I went to the nurses' station and told them I was going to the cafeteria for breakfast. I asked them to call me if anything happened to Jenny.

On my way back from the cafeteria, I decided to stop at the chapel. It was empty, the way I preferred it. I took a seat in my usual chair in the front row. Folding my hands together, I closed my eyes and envisioned Jenny running and laughing on a beach, her white sundress flowing in the breeze. I imagined myself on the beach with her, enjoying a beautiful day as seagulls flew over our heads and dipped down to the water, trying to catch fish. I could feel the warmth of the sun on my face and wished my vision could be real.

"Dear Lord, please bring Jenny back to me. I need her, and I can't live without her. I have faith you'll hear my prayers and answer them." I got up to return to Jenny, and as I walked to the door, something shiny caught my eye. I bent down to get a closer look. With my right hand I picked up a penny, a shiny new penny. I began flipping the penny over and over, admiring its newness. My mind reeled; was this a sign? All at once I could hear my grandmother's voice, singing the song she always sang after my grandfather died when I was twelve: "Pennies from Heaven." She told me whenever she found a penny, she thought that Grampy had left it for her, and looking for pennies helped her get through the days without him. I wondered if this was a sign from my grandfather, telling me everything would be okay. Trusting it was from my grandfather, I put the penny in my pocket and reached for the doorknob.

As I approached Jenny's room, I heard voices talking louder than I had heard in the past; it sounded like many more people than just a nurse and doctor. When I opened the door, I wasn't prepared to see my two children and their grandparents standing next to Jenny's bed. They all turned when the door opened.

"What is going on in here? What is all this?"

"Daddy!" The children ran to me, hugging me around my waist.

"Hey, guys…maybe your grandfathers can take you for a walk so I can talk to your grandmothers." I'm sure my anger showed in my eyes, turning them red.

"Come on, kids. Let's go see if we can get a snack at the cafeteria."

When they had left, I laid into my mother and Ann. "Mom, Ann — what were you thinking? The kids don't belong here. Do you want to scare them? Look at her." I pointed to Jenny.

"Alex, please calm down," my mother said. Ann stood by her side. "We talked about it, Dad and I and Ann and Bob, and we all agreed that the kids should see their mother. You don't know how this is affecting them. They are full of questions, and we are running out of answers."

Ann added, "Alex, we prepared the kids. We told them Jenny is sleeping, and she wouldn't be able to open her eyes and talk to them. They understand she isn't the normal mother they're used to because the doctors gave her medicine to help her sleep, so that her body can heal. We think it's better for them to see for themselves that their mom is alive — not awake but still here. We won't stay long. It's enough for them to just see her and know she is okay."

"'We think'. Well, what about what I think? I don't get it. Why wouldn't you ask me my feelings on this? They're my children."

"Alex, we knew you wouldn't agree. You would want to protect them from seeing Jenny like this. But, son, you don't see the kids every day. You don't have to answer their questions and see the looks on their faces. This hasn't been easy for them, or for any of us. I didn't want to tell you that we were bringing them because I knew you wouldn't agree. I was hoping Jenny would be better by now, but no one knows how long she will live like this, and the kids deserve to see their mother. We can't keep them away forever."

I was angry to hear about the kids' confusion and sorrow about Jenny. "You should have told me they were upset. I could come home more." I exploded, "Ahh, this is killing me, killing all of us." I sat down in the chair and put my head in my hands to think. "I'll be back. I need to cool off. I'm going for a walk."

I knew where to find my family and saw the four of them sitting at a table by window in the cafeteria. Jessica was excited to show me her snack. "Hi, Daddy. Look at what we got." The kids were sharing a huge cinnamon roll and some orange juice.

"Hey, guys. Sorry I was so upset earlier, but you sure did surprise me. Dad, Bob, do you think I could be alone with the kids for a few minutes? We'll see you back at the room."

"Sure, we'll see you there." My father and Bob got up and left the table.

It was about time I talked to the children about the accident and stop dancing around it like it was a fire that would burn me. "So, how are you guys? I haven't seen you in a long time, huh?"

"We are good now that we are eating this. Look at the size of this thing!" Nicolas was more fascinated with his pastry than interested in talking about his mother.

"Yes, Nicolas, I see it. What I really mean is, how are you feeling about Mommy?"

The look in my son's eye told me everything I needed to know. "I miss her, I miss you, and I miss being a family."

"Me too." Jessica kept her eyes on her treat and avoided looking at me.

Fiddling with a napkin, I tried again to connect with the kids, this time with more honesty. "I'm so sorry this happened to us. I wish I could go back to that Sunday afternoon and stop Mommy from leaving, I wish I could yell at the other driver and tell him to get back on his side of the road. But the truth is I can't do any of that. I can't change anything that happened. I can only respond to what is happening." I had their attention. They were both looking me right in the eye.

"I know how hard this is for you guys. Even I can't understand everything that's happening, so I don't imagine how you could." Sunlight showered our table with rays of light. Out the window I saw a red bird take off from a leafless branch. As it flew into the air, I shared its light-ness as I opened up to Nicolas and Jessica about my concerns over them seeing Jenny. It felt right to me to share, just as the bird trusted that it would fly if it stretched out its wings. The bird believed in itself to do what came natural. Suddenly, it felt natural for me to talk to my children. "I'm not sure how I feel about your grandparents bringing you here today. I can't change that either. So I have a question for both of you. How did you feel when you saw Mommy?"

Nicolas spoke first. "When I saw Mommy, I was excited because I really miss her. Then I was sad because she wouldn't wake up to say hi to me. Grammy explained Mommy can't wake up because the doc-tors gave her medicine to make her sleepy so her body can heal." I hated to see the confusion and hurt in my son's eyes.

"I was happy to see Mommy, but she wasn't wearing her pretty clothes. She was wearing the hospital nightgown, and it looks so plain. And then I was sad because she couldn't talk to me. I wanted to hear her say something." Jessica started playing with the ruffle on her skirt.

"Let me share with you what the doctors told me. They said Mommy can hear us, but she can't talk to us because she is really sleepy, but she knows we are with her." I could tell the children under-stood me. "How do you feel about going back to Mommy's room with Daddy? We can all sit around her bed and tell her stories about what's been happening in our lives. You can tell her about school and your sports. I know she would love to hear your voices because she misses you guys too. If she could wake up, I betcha she would tell you how much she misses you." Looking each of them in the eye, I got a good dose of the childhood hope they carried with them. "So what do you think? Will you come back to see Mommy with me?"

"Yes. I want to see Mommy."

"Me too."

"Great, let's go." I gave the naked tree outside the window one last glance, hoping to see that the bird had returned. But he hadn't. He was still enjoying the freedom of flight.

Everyone stopped talking when the kids and I walked into the room. I noticed a candle burning next to Jenny's bed, replacing the antiseptic odor with a scent that reminded me of being at the beach. It was refreshing, one of Jenny's favorite candle fragrances. Ann must have brought it. I asked for some private time with Jenny. After the grandparents left, I invited the children to join me on Jenny's bed. "Here, Nicolas. You can sit here, and Jessica, you can sit on this side. I'll sit right here near Mommy's feet." Nicolas laid his head on his mother's tummy, and with every breath she took his head rose and fell. Watching his head move along with Jenny's breath brought a sense of peace to the room. No one spoke. We enjoyed the peace of being together as a family. Having my family together, even under these circumstances, filled my being with a new calm. "Are you guys okay?"

"We're fine." Nicolas spoke for both of them; they were enjoying the silent company of their mother.

I saw Jessica's fingers rubbing the neckline of the white and blue hospital nightgown her mommy was wearing. "Daddy, why does Mommy have to wear this ugly nightgown?"

"Oh, sweetie, Mommy doesn't mind wearing it. The nurses and doctors need to check Mommy's body, and it's easier for them if she is wearing this type of nightgown." I reached over to soothe her, rubbing her back, and I thought she was right and knew her mother well. Jenny would rather be wearing her own comfortable pajamas.

We spent about forty-five minutes hanging out on Jenny's bed, talking about our days and telling funny stories of things that had happened in our family. I suddenly noticed Jenny's eyes began to twitch; they opened and closed. She had never done that before. Not knowing what would happen next, I questioned if the kids should leave or stay. I sat for the moment and watched to see if the kids noticed what I had seen. They were talking to each other, each one holding one of Jenny's hands. At the same moment, each child pulled away and stared at Jenny's face with a frightened look.

I couldn't figure out what happened. I looked from Nicolas to Jessica, but no one spoke.

"What, guys? What happened?" I got off the bed.

At the same time they said, "She squeezed my hand."

"What? She did? Guys, that's great!"

The kids looked stunned. I told them about the time their grandmother talked to Jenny and she did the same thing, and when I was talking to her, she squeezed my hand.

"This is wonderful! She knows you're here, and that's how she tells us. Mommy can't talk with her mouth, but she can squeeze our hands to tell us she can hear us. You guys are so lucky."

They weren't as excited about it as I was—I think it freaked them out. Sensing they had had enough time with Jenny, I sent them to find their grandparents in the waiting room and to tell them they could return. I watched Nicolas and Jessica walk down the hall to the family waiting room, ecstatic they got to feel their mother move.

Jenny

MY BABIES ARE HERE! OH MY, LOOK AT THEM. I'VE MISSED them. Looking down at the scene playing out in my room, I couldn't believe my eyes. Alex brought the children to the hospital. It was good to see them. I loved having them so close. Nicolas lay on my stomach, and I could smell how sweet he smelled. Jessica still carried the aroma of maple syrup from breakfast. The kids looked very healthy and seemed okay, considering what they must be going through.

"Hi, Nicolas and Jessica! It's Mommy, way up here. I wish you could hear me tell you I love you. I will be okay. I wish you guys could hear my voice."

I loved listening to the stories Alex and the kids were telling. If only I could share my funny family memories.

I want to be part of that world again. I miss my life, and I want them to know that I'm here, that I can hear them, and that I'm okay. I am determined to try to wake up and open my eyes. Then they would know I am going to be okay.

I tried with all my might, but nothing happened. I took a deep breath, refocusing my energy, and was able to flutter my eyes open. As they opened and closed, I saw a different view of the room. I held their little hands tighter in mine. And then they were gone.

I noticed the children get off the bed and leave the room. *Oh no! What happened?* I want them back, their hands in mine. *Where did they go? No, come back. I need to see you.* What happened? What had I done? I'd scared my own children. I only wanted them to know I was okay.

I could feel my husband's body close to mine. As he leaned over my body holding my hand, he whispered in my ear, "Honey, thank you. The kids needed to feel that. They miss you so much. It's been two weeks since your accident. Please, Jenny, wake up and come back to us. We need you, honey." As he whispered into my ear, I wanted to get back to him. I needed them too. I was lonely in this new world. I don't think I will ever forget feeling the love present on the other side of life — seeing my life play out before me like a movie, seeing my grandfather again, and watching my life unfold in the hospital room. But to see my family mourning for me and realize how empty they felt because my injuries kept me unconscious was painful. It hurt me to know I was causing them pain. I experienced a new burning desire like never before. I was determined to wake up. I couldn't go on like this any longer. My family needed me, and I needed them.

After being with my children and family, I was wrapped up in my emotions, enjoying the aroma from the candle next to me. The fragrance stirred up memories of the times I spent at the beach, my favorite place.

I didn't see her approach, but I sensed her presence. When I turned, Aunt Sally greeted me with a tender smile and endearing words.

"Hi, Jenny. Doesn't the beach scent remind you of the days we spent at the beach when you were younger?" She paused for a moment. "I've missed you terribly, but I have been witness to your life. Darling, your children are a beautiful creation from the love you and Alex share. You are the loving mother I always knew you would be, and you possess the natural qualities of a woman who was meant to be a mother. Jenny, they need you. You must move through your obstacles, gather all your strength, and wake up. It's time."

"Aunt Sally, are you really here? Let me touch you." I held her hand and felt a surge of energy pass through her into my hand. It was like she never left me.

"Jenny, I am here. It's good to be with you. You have grown to be an amazing woman who has accomplished so much good in her life. You spread joy to many people through your love, which makes me so proud of you. But you need to go back to your family and friends. You need to finish the life you and Alex started. Your life is not over yet. The man you love is waiting for you to go back to him and experience what else life has in store for you."

"I keep trying to wake up, but it's so difficult. I want to go back, I want to be with Alex and the kids, I do…but I can't."

"Jenny, dear, you have the strength. You must believe in yourself, and then you will wake up."

We held each other. I felt her loving energy pass through me. I found myself crying from the hurt of missing her, but it was healing for me to hold her in my arms again. "I have missed you more than I ever thought possible."

She placed a finger to my lips to shush me. "Jenny, I must say good-bye again. This isn't forever. I will see you again. Many years from now, I will greet you when your time has come to stay by my side and live in eternity with me."

I released her from the life-giving hug. "Thank you, Aunt Sally. I will believe in myself and continue to make you proud." My hands fell to my sides. I stood alone again.

I spun around to watch the room below me.

Alex

I LEANED OVER JENNY'S BODY AND LISTENED TO HER BREATHE. I whispered in her ear, "I miss being close with you. I miss the warmth of your embrace and the softness of your lips on mine." If this was as close to being with her as I could get, I would take it. Breathing in the love we shared, I closed my eyes, remembering how good it felt to be close to her, to feel her lips on mine, her fingers touching my naked chest as our passion intensified. My thoughts started to turn me on. The moment the door opened, I jumped like a teenager about to be caught with his pants down.

"We heard the good news! We had to come see for ourselves. Did she do it again?" Jenny's mother, who had yet to feel her daughter's hand clasp her own, said with excitement. She moved to the side of the bed and picked up her daughter's hand. Looking it over, she kissed the backside. "Hi, Jenny, it's Mom. The kids told me you squeezed their hands. Honey, can you hear me? Jenny?" Waiting for her to respond, Ann brushed Jenny's hair off her face. "Let me know you can hear me." After a minute, she turned to me with a heavy look and said, "Nothing."

"Oh, Ann, it'll happen. It probably took so much of her strength to let the kids know she could hear them. Don't lose hope."

Just then Jenny fluttered her eyes again. "Ann, keep holding her hand."

Ann looked at me, hopeful, and she waited. I watched Jenny's hand and noticed it just barely tighten around her mother's hand. At that moment, I looked up to see tears fall from Ann's eyes. "You heard me. She can hear me. Oh, Jenny dear, I love you, sweetie. We are all here for you. Wake up, Jenny." Ann leaned into Jenny's ear, and whispered, "You can do it. Wake up, Jenny."

As Ann leaned over, whispering in Jenny's ear, she heard, "Mmmuum," ever so soft and jumbled.

Ann turned to us. "Did you hear that? Did anyone hear it? I think she tried to say 'Mom'."

"Yes, Jenny. Yes, it's your mom. I can hear you. I heard you." Sweeping Jenny's hair off her forehead like she was her little girl again, Ann kept talking to Jenny. "You sweet thing, wake up."

Ann touched Jenny's skin; Jenny's eyes were flashing open and closed. I remembered what the nurse told me about coma patients being unable to control their reflexes as they healed from their injuries, but I believed Jenny was trying to keep them open, responding to the voices of our family gathered around her.

Ann said, "Alex, talk to her. Let her hear your voice." She stepped aside. I saw the kids holding onto my mother's waist at the foot of the bed. They looked curious about what was happening to their mother.

"Jenny, we are all here. Honey, can you look right here? Look to where you hear my voice. Jenny?" My face was inches from hers; my eyes darted around her face. I held my breath and waited. The clock on the wall kept time, ticking every second away, and every second that passed felt like minutes. The tension grew as we waited for Jenny to react to my voice. "Jenny, talk to us."

Nothing.

Ann stepped closer to the bed and continued to talk to her daughter; the family gathered closer too. Jenny's eyes were opening and closing, and she turned her head very slightly. We waited, paralyzed, for her to make another move or utter her next word. But nothing happened. After about five minutes, Jessica broke the silence, frustrated. "When is she going to wake up?"

I left Jenny's side to go to Jessica, hoping to calm her. I placed my hands on Jessica's shoulders, and I tried to reassure her. "We don't know, honey, but maybe soon. We need to be patient with Mommy. It's very hard for her right now. She's trying, honey." Jessica looked up at me. With my hands still on her shoulders, I felt how small my daughter really was.

Jenny

I WANT TO SCREAM, "MOM, I DO HEAR YOU," BUT NOTHING WILL come out. I have tried so many times. "Mom, Mom." It takes so much energy, but I am trying.

I wanted to lift my head up from the flat pillow, move my face closer Alex's and kiss his mouth, tell him, "Yes, I hear you, and I want to open my eyes and see you." But I couldn't move. My head was too heavy on the pillow. My eyes were so hard to open they felt like they had been stitched shut.

During those moments when I had been able to move, I was glad my family felt hope that I was alert, but the effort exhausted me. I wanted to say more. I wanted to tell all of them how much I loved them and to let them know I knew they were praying for me. When I realized the amount of strength it took to move a little bit and how tired I was after, I began to worry about how long it would take to re-build my muscles. Before my accident I'd worked out five days a week and had great stamina. I hardly got sick. I hoped being in good shape before would help with a quick recovery.

I knew I had the determination to get back to the life I left more two weeks ago. I badly wanted to be with my family, and nothing was going to stand in my way. I zealously prayed to God to give me the strength to help me move for my family, to recover. It had taken so much strength to move, and I knew I was going to need God's help to fully heal from the accident. I wouldn't be able to do it on my own.

Alex

JENNY WAS SHOWING MORE SIGNS OF ACTIVITY SINCE THE ACCIDENT. The family and I anticipated her waking up at any moment, and everyone wanted to be there so she wasn't alone when she opened her eyes. But the kids were getting restless, and I thought it might be a good idea to get them home. They needed time to process the emotions they were feeling after seeing their unconscious mother in the hospital.

"The doctors say it takes time for her body to recover and wake up. Even though she had a great day today, it doesn't mean today is the day she will open her eyes and talk to us. I think maybe the kids should go home and relax. It's been a big day for them, and they saw a lot." I looked at my mother to back me up.

"Yes, maybe you're right. It has been a lot to take in." My mother caught on.

"No, we want to stay," they said at the same time. "We can't leave. It's not fair that you can stay with her and we have to go."

"Guys, it's not fair, you're right. But you can't stay here all night and day. You need to go to school, see your friends, and play your sports. Mommy wouldn't want you hanging out here all day. It would make her happier to know you are enjoying yourselves rather than moping around the hospital. Please understand I don't want to send you home any more than you want to go."

"When can we come back to see Mommy?" Jessica hugged my leg, looking at her mother lying in bed.

"Well, Nanny and I will figure out a time when you can come back to see Mommy. Maybe in a few days." I rubbed her back and confirmed my words with a nod to my mother.

Ann took both of her grandchildren in her arms. As she held them, she told them, "You two are so understanding. I'm very proud of you, and I bet your mommy is too. It's not easy to be going through all this. You guys seem to be handling it very well. I love you both, very much." She kissed each of their heads. "Your mommy is fighting very hard to wake up. What she did today was very tiring, and we need to let her rest now. You'll be able to come back when the time is right."

"Thanks, Mimi." They smiled, and their little voices were full of pride.

Ann looked over at Jenny and said, "We'll be here all day. We're hoping to see Jenny wake today." She concluded in a fragmented voice, "I miss my daughter."

Bob placed his arm around his wife's shoulders. "In time, my dear."

I walked my parents and children to the car. We made small talk about the kids' week ahead: school work, practices, and the birthday party Nicolas was going to. It sounded like the kids were going to have a great week. When we got to the car, I hugged the kids good-bye and told them how much I loved them. With a heavy heart I watched them drive away, wishing Jenny and I were in the car too.

The breezy night air swept the ground, whisking leaves up and swirling them around in a circle, and I walked back through the parking garage into the hospital. My thoughts wandered to the many fall afternoons I'd spent raking leaves with Jenny and the kids. After we finished, we would go pick pumpkins and apples. Pumpkins… Reality blew through my memories. Would Jenny be home to choose pumpkins? Probably not. It was almost Halloween already, and I didn't even know if the kids had costumes or if I would see them dressed up for Halloween. I hated the thought that we would miss apple and pumpkin picking as a family. The more I worried about it, the more I started to miss home.

Trying to shake my negative thoughts about what we were missing as a family, feeling as though my body would fall to pieces any moment, I walked to the one place I knew would lift my spirits, the chapel.

One woman sat in the back, at the end of the row. It was the first time I'd seen another person in the chapel. I walked to my favorite seat in the front and placed my folded hands on my lap. I spoke to God. "Thank you, Lord, for the many blessings you sent today. It was a surprise to see my children here, but they seemed to handle the situation pretty well. Jenny had a great day, thank you. I pray to you that she wakes up soon, that she is healthy and has no side effects from the accident. I ask you to give me strength for my family, so they can lean on me to comfort them. Thank you, Lord."

I sat for a few minutes enjoying the peace only this room in the hospital could offer me. When I got up to leave, the lady in the back of the chapel stopped me. "Excuse me, sir?"

Confused whether she was talking to me, I turned to look around. Had anyone else come in? But I was the only other person. "Yes?"

Looking me squarely in the eye, she told me, "She'll be okay."

"What? What are you talking about?" I looked at her, confused. I didn't know what to think. Was this lady crazy?

"The person you were praying for…I was told to tell you, 'Soon'." She stood and placed her hand on my arm, squeezed it, and walked out the door.

Stunned, I stood silent for a few seconds, trying to comprehend what she said, before I called out. "Wait. Wait, come back. What do you mean, soon?" I opened the door, but she was gone. The empty corridors went for more than one hundred feet in either direction; there was no way a woman of her stature could have disappeared that quickly.

"Hello?" I yelled in both directions, but no one answered. Under my breath I whispered, "Where did she go? Who *was* that? What did she mean, soon?" *Was that an angel?* I stood there, dazed, for a while before returning to Jenny.

When I opened Jenny's door, the doctor was standing by her bed talking with her parents.

"Oh, hi. Sorry to interrupt." It looked like they were in a deep discussion.

"No, not at all. Come in. I was just telling Jenny's parents about the last MRI and the other tests. They all look great. The swelling is going down considerably. Jenny has been maintaining normal blood pressure readings, oxygenation rates, and body temperature. She's been breathing on her own for some time now. I would like to taper her off the oxygen. We want to see how she does with less help because everything else looks good. We think she can handle it, but we can't know for sure, if we don't try." Dr. Winters was younger than me, but had the disposition of a more mature man. He had a way of earning trust and making us feel comfortable about making decisions. He didn't force his opinions, but instead spoke in a way that led us to feel like we were part of the decision making.

"Well, you're the doctor, and you were right about the ventilator. I trust your judgment." I looked at Jenny's parents for support.

"Yes, we agree."

"Okay, I'll have a nurse come by. We'll start reducing flow slowly." He made a note in Jenny's chart and left the room.

The nurse came by later. With Jenny's oxygen flow lowered, new sounds entered through the door. We could hear nurses' chatter and machines being wheeled past. I welcomed the quiet within the room. Ann, Bob, and I sat around Jenny's bed, talking about the kids and how well they'd handled their visit today. I thanked them for their support with the kids and for supporting me. They shared their appreciation for how loving I was to their daughter and grandchildren. As we talked, we noticed Jenny's breathing. There were periods when she filled her lungs with deep breaths, and the mask helped her when she couldn't do so.

It seemed every day she was getting stronger. We were filled with excitement that she was breathing without full support. She was meeting the milestones the doctors set for her, and we were all so proud of Jenny. It seemed at any moment a new energy would fill her and she would open her eyes and speak to us, but as the hours passed, Jenny's condition didn't change. Ann and Bob decided it was time to leave.

"We'll come back tomorrow around lunch time. That way you can have a break." Then Ann embraced me. "You're starting to feel like skin and bones. You need to eat more, Alex."

"You sound like my mother."

"Well, good mothers think alike." She winked at me.

"I have noticed my pants are starting to hang loose on me, but it's hard to eat when I feel that what I put in my stomach will only come back up. I'm sick to my stomach over what's happening here."

"She would want you to take care of yourself. You need to eat. Look, we can stay a while longer. Go get yourself some dinner," Bob insisted. "Buy two meals, for crying out loud. You need it."

"Thanks. I won't be long." I was happy to go. It would give me a chance to try to find the lady from the chapel.

On the walk to the cafeteria, I looked at every person who walked past me, and I looked at every face in the cafeteria, searching with intensity for the woman from the chapel. If I found her, I wanted to ask her what "soon" meant. I had an idea, but I wanted to hear it from her. But it seemed useless. No one looked like her; she'd had the whitest hair, like the sun, and her eyes were the color of the sky on a clear summer day. But it was her voice that struck me, what haunted me the most. It was like she was singing when she spoke. There was a peaceful tone to it. She had radiated warmth and love.

No one I saw that evening even came close to the person I'd spoken to in the chapel earlier. I wanted so desperately to find her. I kept my head up and checked out person after person on the way back to Jenny's room, but I never found the woman. She remained a mystery.

I had come to welcome the solitude of the hospital. I passed people in the hallways, saying a quiet hello, but no one ever stopped to ask why I was there, and I never asked the same. So many people were moving in different directions with so little conversation.

I entered Jenny's room with a smile, feeling good to be back in the comfort of my new home. "Any changes?" I asked Ann and Bob when I walked through the door.

"No, not yet," Ann said, ever the optimist. "How was dinner?"

"Well, I'm full. That's the important thing. You guys should be hitting the road. It's getting dark. I don't want you driving too late."

"Yes, we should be going. Call us if you need us."

"Will do."

I sat staring at my wife, wondering how many times in all our years together I'd told her I loved her, but no matter how many times I came up with, I sensed I should have told her more often. Did she know how deep my love for her was? I pulled the hospital chair closer to her bed and told her, "I'm going to start at the beginning of the alphabet and tell you what I love about you the most. A, the great advice you give me, even if I don't always use it. B, your brains. You are the smartest person I know. C, the crook of your arm. It's what held our babies and kept them safe, and it's where I rest my head when I lay in your arms." I massaged her arm. "D — that's an easy one. Your dedication to me. You are the one who stood by me through all the hard times in my life, and you gave me time to find my way out of them. You never left when things got bad."

During our college years when I was stressed out over trying to juggle hockey and studying, Jenny was always there, smiling and supporting me. If I was having a bad day, she used it as a challenge to make me smile. When I was in grad school and working full time, she would bring me food or encourage me to take a break in between studying. We often went on walks around my parents' neighborhood or she would pull me away from the library and we would walk around town. During those walks she would fill me in on the wedding details.

I leaned over to kiss her cheek and hoped she could feel it; sitting at her bedside, I was returning the favor she showed to me all those years ago. "E, your eyes. They sparkle like the stars in the night sky. They captivated me the first time I saw you. F, your flirtatiousness. I love how you find ways to subtly turn me on in front of people. You're so good at it." I hovered over Jenny's face. I noticed the bruises and swelling were almost gone, revealing her soft facial features again. "I love you, Jenny. I always have and always will." I sat back in the chair, and then I heard her moan. "What, Jenny? Try it again." I stood up again, so close to her face I could feel the air as it escaped through her oxygen mask.

"Say it again. Try again, Jenny." I waited, and very softly I heard her moan again. "I hear you, Jenny. Oh, God, please talk to me, Jenny. What do you need? I'm right here."

Out of the corner of my eye, I saw Jenny lift a finger slowly, like a flower opening a new bloom. "Hey, you want me to hold your hand?" I would do anything for her if it meant she would talk or move. I gently lifted Jenny's hand into mine; it was so small and fragile. She was losing weight. As I held her hand I thought of the day I'd placed the engagement ring on it. There was never any a doubt about asking her to marry me. I loved her more than anything. I knew she was the one I wanted to spend my life with.

"Jenny, I'm here. Can you hear me?" She held my hand in hers a little tighter. "Jenny. Oh, my sweet Jenny. Wake up and open your eyes. I miss seeing those sparkling brown eyes. Can you hear me? Jenny, you can do it. Wake up." My heart raced as she made another attempt to wake up. It was happening — she was coming back to me.

Jenny

My eyes started to flutter. My hand trembled in his, and I was able to make the smallest of sounds, like a newborn baby. I was fighting so hard to open my eyes, but every time I tried was harder than the first. I could hear him talking to me and I wanted to tell him, but I couldn't. My tongue was too heavy, like it was weighted down and stitched to the inside of my mouth. I wanted to move my body, reach for his hand and kiss it, like he has done to me so many times. I thought I was moving but it must have been in slow motion. The movements were hard to make, like I was stuck in mud.

I was determined to let him know I was here. I had to at least say his name. "Aa…l…" It was like I had thick honey on my tongue. My tongue was so heavy I could barely move it. "Aallx." Almost. I took a deep breath and waited for a moment. With more intensity I pushed through the weight. "Allexx." I did it, it was out. I had to try again. "Al-lexx."

I could feel my muscles wake up; a new sensation was taking over my body. I was coming back into my body. When I spoke I felt warmer, like I was controlling my body. I wanted to say more, I didn't want to stop. "I…" I said it drawn out, like I was talking in slow motion. It was harder than I thought. "I…lluv…ouuu." I was speaking! I was doing it. He heard me, and I knew it because I felt his hand squeeze mine.

His other hand was on my head, brushing my hair back. His touch was magical. It felt so invigorating to be touched by him. I didn't want him to stop. I realized I was feeling it, not watching from above — feeling every one of his caresses. It was amazing. My skin tingled, and I felt goose bumps rise on my arms when he touched them. He was healing me with every touch. His touch on my face made it come alive with warmth. He rubbed my shoulders, and it relaxed them. Then he went back to my head and moved his fingers around on my scalp. With every touch, I felt energy racing through my body. I felt electrified, and I tingled from my head down to my toes. The place his lips had been on my cheek carried a new sensation of warmth, like the after-burn from a bee sting. I was filling up on his love. Every time he touched me, my skin trembled from the strong sensations.

I could hear him speak to me with encouragement, asking me to open my eyes. I tried, but my lids were too heavy. I wanted to open them so I could see his face, look into his eyes. I knew if I could look into his eyes they would tell me everything would be okay. I fought to open my eyes against the heaviness of my eyelids, and I started to see things. The images were blurry at first, and then the edges became sharper. Alex's face came into focus. He was smiling from ear to ear and saying my name. It was like I was waking up from a dream. His voice was muffled at first, but the more he said my name the clearer it became.

The sound of his voice relaxed me and slowed the adrenaline that had been rushing though my veins. I turned my face to meet his; using the last drop of energy I said, "Aallex. I missed you." And, a lonely tear fell from the corner of my eye. I used all my strength to get the words out, and I felt like I had climbed the tallest mountain and reached the summit to see the world in every direction. At that moment, I knew everything was possible.

Alex

"JENNY! JENNY, I HEAR YOU. I'M RIGHT HERE. I LOVE YOU TOO, honey. Oh, I can't believe you're talking! It's so good to hear your voice. It's music to my ears. I have missed it, and I've missed you, but you came back—you're back. Thank you, Lord. Thank you." I spoke quickly; I had to get everything out. "Jenny, I've been praying—you wouldn't believe it. I understand the power of prayer now. Jenny, all these years you've been trying to tell me about God and praying and I thought you were nuts, but I get it now. I see the way it works. It's easier to ask for help than to force what you want. I have found it so powerful not to have to be in control of everything. At times it's hard, but I'm working on it. I have surrendered, Jenny. I'm sorry I ever doubted you. He brought you back to me—God brought you back."

I kept stroking her scalp and kissing her cheeks. It was a shock to see Jenny awake, and my emotions were all over the place. I looked around, wishing someone was to here to witness this, to tell me I wasn't delusional. My prayers had been answered, and I was in my glory because Jenny was awake. My hands and lips moved all over her face. I removed the oxygen mask and kissed her on her lips. Pulling back, I saw the corners of her mouth turn up. My wife was back.

I grabbed the bedside remote and called for the nurse. "Jenny's awake. Come quickly." Facing the door, I waited for the doctor to open it and race in, but instead my eye caught the calendar hanging on the wall next to the cabinet and sink. Today was October 22. The date seemed strangely familiar to me, but I couldn't figure out the significance.

After a moment I turned to Jenny, thinking about the date. I remembered how nervous she had been that I would suffer the same fate as Ben. Then it hit me—I knew the date's importance. The memories about the nightmares she had been having over the last year washed over me. I remembered the one she told me about, with the image of a dark office and the cryptic calendar on the desk. Jenny thought her dream meant I was going to die on October 22, but actually it was the date she would come back to me.

Dr. Winters and the nurse walked in and interrupted my observations. He gave Jenny an examination. "This is all good news, Alex. She is able to open and close her eyes when I instruct her to, her reflexes are strong, she responds to hot and cold compresses, and she is able to move all parts of her body. This is nothing short of a miracle, I would say. During the next twenty-four hours I will have the team of doctors on Jenny's case come by to continue her evaluation. She should be allowed to sleep tonight—no visitors. You can call your family, but I would advise against them coming in at this hour."

"Of course, doctor. May I ask you a question? Do you think this is it—she's okay? She's going to be okay?" I needed to hear him say that Jenny was going to live.

"I think your wife is going to be just fine." He gave me a reassuring pat on my arm.

When the doctor left the room, I returned to Jenny. I hadn't fully absorbed that she had woken up and talked to me. Now she was resting again, her eyes closed, her breathing even. The nurse turned the oxygen down and removed the mask, leaving the nose piece. Without the mask I could see Jenny's whole face. I was amazed at how well she'd healed from the cuts and bruises. I enjoyed seeing her face, and all I wanted to do was kiss her. I kissed her lips, I kissed her nose. I kissed her forehead. I kissed every part of her face I'd missed seeing. I realized that over the last two weeks there was a lot I'd missed about Jenny.

"Jenny, I am going to call your parents and my parents, and I have to visit a special place, but I won't be too long. Rest, my darling, and I will be back very soon." As the word came out of my mouth, I froze. *Soon*, I thought. That's what the lady in the chapel said—she said, "She'll be okay. Soon."

I spoke out loud. "She knew! She meant that you would wake up soon. She had to be an angel." I jumped when I felt Jenny's hand touch my hand. It was going to take time for me to get used to her touching me again. "Jenny, I'm sorry. Did I wake you?"

"Ang...el?" Her voice was very weak.

"Yes, I said angel. I think I saw an angel today in the chapel. She told me you would be okay. And then she said 'soon' and disappeared out the door. It has freaked me out all day. I've been looking for her. I haven't been able to find her, but I know why—she's an angel." The word hung in the air as Jenny drifted off to sleep. *Angel, angel.* The word kept echoing in my mind.

I went outside and called Jenny's parent first.

"Hi, Ann, it's Alex. I need Bob to get on the phone too." Misty frost vapors poured out of my mouth with every word.

"Is everything all right, Alex?"

"Yes, everything is great. Is Bob there?"

"Hi. I'm here."

"Are you both on the line?"

"Yes, we are. What's going on?"

"It's happened. She's awake. Jenny's awake! It happened a couple of hours ago. I was talking to her, telling her how much I loved her, and she started to make noises and she moved her hand. It was amazing. It all happened very slowly, but she's awake. I can't believe it."

"Oh my God, it's a miracle. Bob, can you believe it?"

"I'm speechless. I need a minute."

"Alex, did the doctor check on her?" Ann asked.

"Yes, Ann. He came in to see her and he said she looks great. Her reflexes are strong and her breathing is stronger, too, so they removed the oxygen mask and put in a nose piece. You can see her face again. She looks beautiful."

"Alex, should we come in?" Bob's voice sounded composed.

"No, Bob, not tonight. Dr. Winters said she should get a good night's rest. She can have visitors tomorrow. She is still weak. She's sleeping now." I shook my head—I couldn't believe the words coming out of my mouth, "I just can't believe she's awake."

"It's great news. Did you call your parents?"

"No, I called you first."

"Call them. They will want to know the great news—they can tell the kids in the morning."

"Thanks, Ann, I will. I'll see you in the morning?"

"Yes, we'll come in after breakfast."

"Good night, guys."

I looked up at the clear night sky and admired all the twinkling stars while I waited for someone at my parents' house to answer the phone. I shared the news with my parents; they were ecstatic. My mother told me the children were in bed sleeping, so in the morning she would tell them that their mother was awake.

"Mom, call the school in the morning and tell them the kids wouldn't be going. I want the whole family together to enjoy the good news." I felt strongly that the kids needed to be with Jenny, to see her awake and hear her voice.

"I will. We will head into the hospital right after breakfast. Alex, your prayers were answered." My mother's voice sounded dignified.

"I know, Mom. It's a blessing."

I had one more stop to make before returning to Jenny. I had visited the chapel every one of all the days I spent at the hospital. There, I prayed for Jenny to wake up and be healthy. Now it was time for a different prayer. I needed to give thanks to God because my prayers had been answered.

As I walked to the chapel this time, a different feeling was taking place in me. With all my being, I truly wanted to go pray—not so much a prayer as a thanksgiving. I wanted to run into the chapel, drop to my knees, and yell out to God, "Thank you, thank you!"

I approached the door to the chapel and took a deep breath. As I entered, I was glad to see I was alone. I sat in my usual seat, and raw emotions took over my body; I couldn't hold back or stop them. I began to recall all the times I'd sat there before, never knowing if Jenny would wake up or not. Today she had. I was overcome with joy. Tears fell from my eyes. My body shook from the adrenaline, and I tried to calm myself down so I could speak, but I couldn't stop my tears, so I spoke in broken words. "Lord, I have come to you for more than two weeks, praying for my wife to wake and be healthy, and tonight Jenny woke up from her coma. She spoke to me, and she touched me. I don't know how I could have gotten through this without believing your strength would keep me strong. I put all my faith in you, and you didn't let me down. Thank you. I'm sorry for being stubborn in the past, but I didn't know how to let myself go and let you in. I know now, and I won't turn away from you again." I sat for a few minutes, enjoying the stillness. I felt the weight lift off my shoulders. My wife was going to be okay. Soon enough, we would be together again as a family.

My parents and children arrived at the hospital bright and early the next morning.

"Hey, guys. You're here nice and early."

"Well, we couldn't keep them away once we told them their mom was awake." My mother gave me a big hug before the kids ran up to me, practically knocking me over, and we all hugged. Then we went over to Jenny's bed. I held my kids close as we looked at Jenny.

"She isn't awake just now. She had peaceful sleep last night. I heard her moving a little.

"Nicolas, Jessica, look here." I stood by Jenny's bed, one child on either side of me. I showed them the oxygen mask had been removed and explained the little plastic tube in their mother's nose helped her get more oxygen.

"That's cool." It intrigued Nicolas, who was more interested than Jessica.

Jessica melted my heart when she looked up at me with her brilliant blue eyes and asked, "Can I talk to her? Will she hear me?"

"Yes, definitely. Tell her you love her and that you miss her."

"Hi, Mommy, it's Jessica. Can you hear me? I love you, Mommy. I miss you too." Her voice sounded soft, like a flower petal. "Please, Mommy, wake up."

In response to Jessica's voice, I saw Jenny move her finger, just as she did last night. "Jessica, look, she is moving her finger—she hears you."

Jessica held her mommy's hand and rubbed it. Then she planted a wet kiss on her cheek. "Mommy, you can hear me. Daddy said you woke up last night. I'm so proud of you." She turned when everyone in the room chuckled.

"Well, I am." Jessica looked back at her mommy and kept encouraging her to open her eyes.

Nicolas walked over to the other side of the bed and took hold of his mother's other hand. "Hi, Mommy, it's Nicolas. I'm here too, and so are Nanny and Grandpa. We've been sleeping at their house. We didn't go to school today, so we could come see you. I'm so happy you woke up. I love you." He whispered so softly in her ear we could barely hear.

As the children talked to their mother, she was able to move her hands and squeeze their hands. After about fifteen minutes of talking to and touching Jenny, she started to open her eyes and look around the room. She glanced at both children and then at me before shutting her eyes again.

"Why can't she keep them open?" Jessica was confused.

"Honey, it's a lot of hard work for Mommy to use her muscles. She's been laying here sleeping for more than two weeks and she's weak. We need to be patient with her. Understand she wants to keep them open, but it's hard for her."

"Mommy, you can do it. Open your eyes." Jessica was cheering her on.

We continued to watch Jenny as she fought against the weight of her eyelids. She opened her eyes a few more times and looked at her daughter. Jessica was thrilled when she saw her mother look into her eyes and smile at her. "Daddy, did you see that? Did you see her? She smiled at me."

"I did, Jessica, I did. She's trying, sweetheart. She's trying." I was overcome with pride for my wife, and I held back my tears. I knew she could do it; she was the strongest person I knew.

"Good job, Jenny. We're all here, honey. Open your eyes. You'll see the kids, my parents, and me. We are waiting to talk to you."

Just as the words came out of my mouth, the door opened, and Jenny's parents and brother came into the room.

"Hi, everyone. How's she doing?" Ann walked over to the bed.

"Hi, Mimi." Jessica hugged her grandmother.

"She's responding to the kids. She hasn't spoken yet, but she opened her eyes and moved her hand."

Hoping Paul would get a strong response, I told him to come talk to his sister. "Maybe she'll respond to you."

"Hi, Jenny. It's Paul. I came back to see you because I heard you opened your eyes and talked to Alex. Jenny, can you talk to me? Mom and Dad are here too. Talk to us, Jenny. We want to hear your voice."

I watched Jenny try to open her eyes to look at Paul, as she had the night before with me. And then Paul noticed the corner of her mouth pull back, as if she tried to smile. "Come on, Jenny, you can do it."

"P…Pa…l."

"Yes, Jenny! It's me, Paul."

Everyone in the room cheered. I looked at my mother and Ann as they wiped the tears that rolled down their cheeks. We all looked at each other, full of happiness. "Jenny, you did it." Paul was fighting back his tears.

"Yeah…" she said with a half-smile.

Ann and Bob embraced. "She's going to be okay."

As the day progressed, Jenny spoke a few more times. Nicolas and Jessica were happy to hold her hands, and they were thrilled when she smiled at the stories they told her. Observing them interacting with Jenny again made it easy to see they loved their mother very much. Seeing with their own eyes that she was getting stronger and would be better soon reassured them.

"Daddy, when can Mommy come home?"

"Well, we will have to wait for the doctors to decide that. She still has a lot of work ahead of her before she is running after you two." I grabbed Nicolas's head and messed his hair up.

I overheard our mothers. "It's good to see her moving and trying to talk," my mother said to Ann. "It feels good to have the whole family surrounding her today."

"I love being able to communicate with her, even though it isn't how most people talk. It's been so long since I've heard her voice. And she moved her fingers and held hands to respond to our questions. Yes, she mumbled most words — I know her speech is weak, but it will be stronger in time."

"She's a strong girl, Ann. She can only get stronger." Looking over at Jenny, my mother smiled.

"Oh, Mary, we needed this day. Alex needed this and, my goodness, the kids needed this. I feel like anything is possible now. She's going to be fine. I guess we'll have to wait and see how strong her legs are, but for now, I'm thrilled she is awake and responding to touch."

My mother put her arm around Ann's shoulders. "We all are."

After everyone left for the day I sat on the side of Jenny's bed. "Jenny, I'm so proud of you. You had a great day. The kids are so happy and relieved to know you are going to be okay."

"All…ex, I…lllo…v…yyouu."

Tears fell from my eyes. "Oh, Jenny. You don't even know how much I love you. I couldn't even begin to tell you. You scared me. I thought I had lost you forever. The thought of not having you in my life, of living day and night without you by my side…I think I've aged twenty years in the last two weeks."

I brushed her hair away from her forehead and kissed it. "I never want to feel that way again." I picked up her hand and held it in my own, noting how fragile and tiny it was. "I want to grow old with you. We have so much left to see and experience in life. But first we need to work on getting you stronger. Tomorrow more doctors are coming by to evaluate you. We may need to move you to another facility. You are probably going to need a lot of physical therapy. But someone will always be with you. We won't let you be alone." I kissed the back of her hand.

The next morning, Dr. Winters came by with Nurse Rita. "Good morning, Alex. How's my patient?" I got up to shake his hand and said hello to Rita.

"She had a great night. The family came yesterday, and she was able to open her eyes, move her hands, and say a few words. Everyone was so excited." I was ecstatic to share the news.

"That's great to hear. Let me check her out. Is she awake?" Dr. Winters stood by the bed, his flashlight ready to check her pupils.

"I think she is trying to wake up, but it happens very slowly."

"Jenny, its Dr. Winters. Jenny, can you hear me?"

"Mmm…"

"Good." The doctor seemed impressed by her ability to communicate. "Good morning. I heard you have been able to open your eyes. Can you open them for me now?"

I stood, frozen, watching Jenny. Silently, I was cheering her on. *Come on, Jenny, you can do it.* Then I saw the skin around her eyes move. She was trying to open them; her eyelids started to flutter. I noticed it always happened the same way. First, her eyelids would flutter, then open for a second, then close, and then she could open and try to focus. She looked up at the doctor.

"Good, I see you can hear me and respond to my requests. Very good." He took hold of Jenny's hand. "Jenny, I would like you to squeeze my hand. Go ahead, with all your strength."

Again, I waited and said a prayer in my mind. *You can do it, Jenny.* When she did, I looked at Rita. We were both smiling.

"Umm, very nice. Jenny, that was good." Dr. Winters turned to me. "She is making really good progress. She was able to make a vocal sound, open her eyes, and squeeze my hand. These are all great signs." He walked away from the bed. "I will have some therapists come by today. The nurse may have told you. They will check her muscle strength and speech. Medically, she is good—her vitals are strong. The oxygen could be removed today as well. We'll do another MRI today. I'm thinking the findings on it will be clear, and at this point, I expect most of the bleeding and swelling should be gone. After the therapists report their findings, I will talk with you about transporting her to a rehabilitation facility. There are many to choose from, but I would suggest one close to home." I couldn't agree more with the doctor.

By late morning both therapists had come to check on Jenny. It was determined that she would need occupational and physical therapy, which did not surprise me. I knew she still had a lot more work to do. It didn't bother me, though. She would be closer to home and the kids could visit her every day. It was the closest thing I had to having my family back together.

Jenny's parents came by just as she was taken away for her MRI. "Ann, Bob, I want to show you something. Let's go for walk." I walked them down to the chapel. "Have you guys been here yet?" I could tell by the look on their faces they hadn't.

"Come inside—it's so peaceful. I've been coming here since Jenny arrived." I opened the door. "It's been very helpful in straightening out my thoughts. I never knew what peace praying could bring. With all that has happened, I know now."

"Well, Alex, I can see you're a changed man. Jenny will be very proud of you." Ann touched my arm. "Let's pray."

When we got back to Jenny's room, we found her tucked in bed and propped up with some pillows. She looked beautiful, but I couldn't help notice that my wife was a much skinnier version of the woman I had always loved. I also noticed the oxygen tube was gone; the room was a lot quieter.

As we approached the bed Jenny's eyes opened, which scared me. It was going to take me some time to get used to that.

"Hi, honey." I held her hand.

"Hi, Jenny, it's Mom and Dad." Ann and Bob stood on the opposite side of the bed. All of us gathered around, staring at Jenny, waiting to see how she would respond.

"Jenny, it must feel good to have the tubes out of your nostrils. You look good." Touching her head, I noticed her hair was greasy. "Maybe we can shampoo your hair later? I'll have Rita help me bathe you. I bet you would like it." She smiled at me and closed her eyes.

"Jenny, you are going to be moved soon to a rehabilitation center closer to home. Doesn't that sound great?" Ann voice gave away her excitement about having Jenny closer to home.

"Yeah…"

I explained, "They will work with you, helping you learn how to take care of yourself again. It will be close to our home, so the kids and all the family can come to visit you there. And once you are strong and can walk, I bet then you can come home with me." I felt her squeeze my hand. I guess she liked what she heard.

"Jenny, you are doing so well, honey. We love you so much." Ann leaned in to kiss the forehead of the daughter who brought immense joy to her life.

"We're so proud of you, Jenny. We need to leave now and help Mary and Tom with Nicolas and Jessica, but we'll check in with Alex later." Bob kissed the top of Jenny's head. "Good-bye, sweetie."

I hugged Ann and Bob good-bye and walked them to the door. Our moods had changed in the last couple of days. We knew Jenny would live and that only time stood in the way of her walking and talking again. We stood by the door saying good-bye. I laughed to myself to think that this room had, in a sense, become my home. It was small, not too unlike our first apartment, and it lacked a kitchen, but it had become home to me — my home with Jenny.

Jenny continued to grow stronger every day. I never left her side. As her muscles grew stronger, the doctor and the therapist wanted her to try a liquid diet through a straw. Before she could move to the rehabilitation center, it was important to get her digestive track working again. I started helping her eat. It reminded me of when we fed our babies, but instead this was my wife. It wasn't easy or clean, but after a couple days, she got better at it.

I held the container and placed the straw to her lips. All she had to do was use the muscles in her mouth to bring the liquid up the straw into her mouth and swallow. So effortless for most people, but a real challenge for her. I never knew exactly how much of the liquid made it into her stomach. Streams of the fluid rolled down her chin, but we always emptied the container and enjoyed a laugh about it.

We were able to move to pureed food next, just like we had when we introduced our kids to solid foods. Jenny was starting over and had to relearn everything from the beginning. As I fed her, I started to realize how much work we had ahead of us. Thinking about it only made me want to help her more. This was the woman I loved, and I knew she would have done it for me. I would cheer her on until she was at the finish line, back home again, living her normal life. I reminded myself of the vows I took many years ago — for better or worse, in sickness and in health — and I intended to stand by those words and help her fight to the end.

When I was told Jenny would be discharged from the hospital, I had a hard time believing she was one step closer to coming home. On one hand, during the weeks I spent shuttling around the hospital, feeling secure that Jenny's care was the best, it seemed impossible to think about being anywhere else. But I missed my home, a place I'd left abruptly when the cop showed up at my door, the place that cradled my family and kept us together.

When the day came to leave the hospital, I felt like I was coming apart inside. I was scared to leave. It had become a safety net for me. As long as Jenny was there, I knew she was going to be okay; if she needed anything it would be provided for her with the utmost care. Everything I needed was there: food, showers, nurses, the chapel, and Jenny, all under one roof. But it was time to go. Jenny's nurses and doctors came to say good-bye and wish her a quick recovery.

"Jenny, you have been a delight. You have a beautiful family and a very loving husband. Most of them don't stay with their wives or families the whole time, but this guy," Rita poked my ribs, "we couldn't get rid of him." Rita admired Jenny's will and had become one of Jenny's biggest supporters. She leaned over to hug Jenny, who was lying on a gurney.

Rita turned to me with a nod and a smile; she was crying, so I spoke. "Oh, Rita, what would I have done without you? Our conversations saved me from a lot of heartache. Thank you for letting me turn to you for help. You're an angel." I wrapped my arms around her. "I'm going to miss you and all your help, but this means Jenny is getting better, so I have to admit that to myself and know it is good to move on. Thank you for everything you've done for her—" I placed my hand on Jenny's shoulder — "and for me." Rita was too emotional to reply. She hugged me one last time and walked away.

One by one, we said good-bye to the team of people who'd kept my wife alive and kept me sane. I would never forget the wonderful things they each did, in their own unique ways, to help Jenny heal from the trauma of her accident and offer me support during the challenging times.

I stood in the sunshine, the warmth of the sunrays penetrating my jacket, warming me from the outside in, and watched as Jenny was loaded into the ambulance for the ride to the rehabilitation center. When the EMTs shut the doors and drove off, I turned to go back into the hospital. There was one place I had to visit before leaving for good.

When I entered the room, I couldn't help but notice how my feelings had changed compared to how I had felt the first time I visited the chapel. That time I felt unsure, but now I felt welcomed, confident, knowing I wouldn't be judged and I could speak from my heart. That place, that room, had become a rock for me, my place of solitude. I went there to sit in silence and to pray when I thought things weren't possible, and it changed me. I needed to say one last thank you to the invisible yet overpowering God I had prayed to every day and say good-bye to the place that consoled me when I was at my weakest.

"Lord, thank you. Thank you for returning my Jenny to me and our family. I will continue to help her recover and heal. Thank you for answering our prayers." As I rose to my feet, I felt overjoyed that I had welcomed prayer and faith into my life. Giving the room one more glance, I smiled and turned the doorknob and then walked out.

Alex

WITH JENNY IN THE REHABILITATION CENTER, I WAS ABLE TO return to work and to my life. I had let go of many things while sitting at Jenny's bedside.

I arrived at work around eight-thirty. My desk was drowning under the paperwork that had been accumulating since Jenny's accident. Even though my co-workers pitched in to take over most of my work demands, there were some issues only I could solve.

It felt refreshing to be working, living my life again. The kids and I had a new routine that seemed suitable for us. In the morning, before my feet touched the floor, I would say a prayer to God that my family and I would have a good day. It helped me to remember my priorities and stay connected to Him. Next I started the laundry. After making breakfast and packing snacks and lunches, I sent the kids off to school. I never realized how much work Jenny did just to get the kids ready and out the door in the morning. After school, we tackled homework and then raced to and from practices and visiting Jenny. By bedtime, I crashed. I could never again take for granted how Jenny had managed all the daily responsibilities, always sounding happy when I called to check in.

As the workday wound down, I was shocked at how quickly it had passed. I felt relief when I could see a section of bare wood on my desk; I was getting through my workload. At three o'clock I wrapped up for the day. Before meeting the kids at home, I stopped by the florist to buy a dozen of Jenny's favorite pink and purple roses. I knew nothing cheered Jenny up more than roses.

After I met the kids at the house and drove them to their practices, we went to see Jenny. Her temporary new home was three miles from our house. We were fortunate to have a wonderful in-patient rehabilitation center in our town; it meant our families could visit her as often as they liked. She worked hard every day to regain muscle strength and her voice.

When we got to the rehabilitation center, the kids ran ahead of me.

"Hi, Mommy." Jessica ran into the room.

Nicolas followed her. "Jessica, you're not supposed to run in here. Hi, Mom."

"H…llo, m…onkeys." Jenny's speech was slow, but that didn't stop her from talking. "Wh…ere's Da…ddy? Arrr you here a…l-lone?"

The kids looked at each other and chuckled. "No. He's coming."

Less than a minute after the kids charged into Jenny's room, I walked in to find them gathered around Jenny, showing her the artwork they made for her.

"Hi, honey. I brought these for you." I handed her the flowers and kissed her head.

"Hi, Al…ex, they are gor…geous. Ju…st what this room needs. It la…cks c…olor."

"How do you feel today? You look great."

"I feel so m…uch bet…ter. Wa…tch this."

Jenny rose from her chair all by herself, and she stood without holding onto anything for support. I couldn't believe my eyes.

"Jenny, look at you! That's awesome—you must be so proud." I walked over to her, and I looked into her eyes to see the sparkle that had captured me all those years before. I kissed her on the mouth and then whispered, "I love you."

The kids cheered her on. "Go, Mommy!" Nicolas and Jessica knew how much time their mother had put into working on standing up on her own. It was great for them to see she was making progress and to know how strong she was and that she wasn't a quitter.

We enjoyed spending time together with Jenny, even if it had to be at the rehab center. We appreciated every minute with her. Most nights we stayed until the kids' bedtime. We helped tuck Jenny into her bed.

"Mommy needs her sleep, too. Come on, guys, let's pack up."

"Mommy, in four days we won't have to leave you anymore. Daddy told us you'll be home with us." Jessica leaned over to hug her mother.

"Oh, Jes…sica, I can't wait. I can't im…a…gine how m…uch this has aff…ected you. But I'll be home real soon." She spoke slowly to get the words out without mumbling.

"Come here, Nic…olas, give me a hug. You're not too old to do that, are you?" Jenny's face showed the pleasure she felt to be able to wrap her arms around the children.

"One la…st hug. Come here, Da…ddy."

"I could get used to this," I whispered in her ear. "I have missed you so much. It feels so good to hold you and feel your arms around me." I pulled from the embrace and looked deep into her eyes. "I love you so much, and I can't wait to get you out of here." I placed a gentle kiss on her lips.

"Al…ex, I'm so…rry for what you have gone thr…ough. Thank you for ta…king care of me. I wou…ldn't have wan…ted an…y…one else with me." She placed her hands on my cheeks. "I love you too." Her speech was really slow, but smooth. "I al…ways have."

We stared into each other's eyes and got lost in the moment of being with each other, as the kids groaned behind us with impatience. "Let's go, Dad."

"Okay, okay, I'm coming." I didn't want to leave Jenny's side, but I gave her one more kiss and said good night.

A couple of nights later, my parents took Nicolas and Jessica to dinner to give me time to visit with Jenny alone. I stood in the doorway to Jenny's room. She was sitting in the chair by the window. I was glad we were able to get her a private room; it was comfortable and quiet. The walls were soft white; a pink chair in the corner and a blue night-stand helped to bring color to the otherwise barren room. The curtains hanging from the rod complemented the pink and blue of the furni-ture. Pictures of floral bouquets hung on the walls; the color choices would suit either a man or woman, but the coziness of a real home was missing.

I noticed Jenny's radiance was returning, and I could see the spar-kle glowing in her eyes again. As her muscle strength improved, her movements had become more fluid. I was astounded by her ability to sit up in the chair. It didn't seem that long ago that she could barely lift her head off a pillow. As I stood in the door way admiring her progress, she turned to me.

"Well, are you going to just stand there or are you coming in?" Her voice was still weak, but her words were beginning to blend together. A smile spread on her face as I walked closer to her. A warmth filled me from within as I saw my wife coming back to me. Oh, I had missed her.

"Hi, you. I thought these flowers would brighten up the room." I placed the yellow roses on the table next to the chair and I saw the bouquet of pink and purple roses next to Jenny's bed. Other bouquets from friends and family were beginning to fade, a testament to the time Jenny had been in the rehab center.

I kissed Jenny on the head before I sat in the chair across from her. We talked about the time she spent in the hospital. She had been hav-ing a hard time remembering the accident and being in the hospital.

Speaking slower than most people, she made an effort to speak smoothly as she shared what she could remember. "The whole acci-dent is really a blur to me. All I can remember is the car coming at me, and that's it. The time in the hospital comes back to me in chunks of vivid images I try to put together, like a puzzle, but the pieces don't fit." She played with the zipper on her sweatshirt. "There is a woman who haunts me, though. Was there a nurse who had really blond hair and fair skin? I kept seeing her in my dreams when I was unconscious. Her presence seemed very important. I felt a strong to attraction to her."

"I can't remember anyone fitting that description. There was one nurse in the beginning who was blond. But she was only there for one shift. What else do you remember about the woman? Maybe talking about her will help you remember more."

Jenny explained. "I felt comforted by her. She had a warmth that my body desired, and I felt safe with her. I can remember walking alongside her, although she didn't move quickly. It was more like we were floating. Uh, I don't know—this all sounds so silly." I could tell Jenny was bothered that she couldn't recall why this woman's memory was haunting her.

Reaching out to hold her hand, I encouraged her. "Jenny, give it time. You can't force yourself to remember everything. Dr. Winters said some memories will come back and others will take time. You might not be able to remember everything. Please, go easy on yourself."

"Alex, it's so frustrating to sit here and know I have no memory of almost three weeks of my life." She stared at the sun-yellow roses, and I saw a tear fall from her eye. She wiped the traces of it away with the tip of her finger. "Maybe if you share your memories, it will help clear mine up."

I knew at some point I was going to have to relive everything and feel the emotions I'd tried to hide from her. I was uncomfortable with the idea, but I would do anything to help Jenny. I took a deep breath and started. "In the beginning we didn't know if you were going to live or die. The first week is a blur to me. My memories are of all the tests you had, the new bruises that showed up every day, and times when you lost consciousness. So much changed—every minute of the day, it seemed. I have a hard time remembering the details."

I shifted in my chair, feeling uneasiness take over when I was reminded of the darker emotional days I spent in the hospital. I couldn't look at her; it made the emotions too powerful. Instead I looked down at my folded hands, trying to keep them still. "The first time you lost consciousness I wasn't with you; your parents were. That was only a few hours after you were in the hospital. It was the first time I remember thinking that you could die. It could be possible to lose you. And then I became a mess. I refused to leave your side, fearing at any moment you would take your last breath." I had to stop—it was too much to relive almost losing her. When I looked over at Jenny, tears were flowing down her cheeks. *What a dope I am for upsetting her like this.* I moved by her side.

"Honey, are you okay? I'm so sorry. I shouldn't have gone on like that."

"No, it's okay." She wiped her cheeks dry. "I remembered the first time I saw the woman. Alex, I think she was an angel."

"What are you talking about? You saw an angel?" *She must be confused.* I wondered if they'd switched her medication.

"Alex, I know you don't believe in these things, but I do. I saw her, and I talked to her. She was with me when all this was happening to me; she never left me. I remember now—it's starting to come back to me. Not everything, but I can remember who she is. She was my guardian angel." She said it with confidence, but I didn't know if I should believe her.

"Jenny, this all sounds too weird to me. What are you talking about? Next you're going to tell me you had an out-of-body experience." I was downplaying Jenny's impression of seeing an angel, but hearing what she said shook me. I hadn't spoken to Jenny about the woman I saw in the chapel since she first woke up, but I was beginning to think maybe it was the same woman —Jenny's guardian angel.

"I won't tell you that. Instead I will share with you what I saw and how I felt."

Jenny

"I WAS DRIVING HOME FROM THE GROCERY STORE AFTER BUYING the mushrooms I needed for dinner. The radio was on, and I was thinking about the week ahead. Halloween was coming, and I needed to get the kids' costumes. Nicolas wanted to be a cowboy, and Jessica wanted to be a ballerina. I noticed the car approaching me. It appeared the driver was looking down and then up at the road. He must have been driving faster than I realized, because before I knew it the car was driving straight at me. I didn't have time to stop. I panicked, and as I moved my foot to push the brakes, I hit the accelerator and pulled the steering wheel away from the oncoming car. I screamed out loud. I knew it was too late. The car was heading toward the tree in front of me, and I was going to hit it. I had nowhere else to go. There was nothing I could do.

"The next thing I remember is being in the hospital. I could see the room I was in, but I noticed I was higher than everyone else.

"I could hear you talking to me. I could see you, and I knew you and our families were hurting so much. I wanted to talk to you, but no matter how hard I tried to speak, I couldn't make a sound. That's when I felt the angel next to me. The first time I looked at her I saw her blond hair and fair skin, and then she morphed into a radiant aura. She turned from being human to being a soul." I wanted so badly for Alex to believe me, because I knew that had really happened to me, but he kept looking at me with a puzzled expression.

I continued with my story. "There was a movie screen that showed images of my life, from pictures of my childhood to an image of us as an elderly couple sitting on a porch swing. At that point I knew I wasn't going to die. I got to see the future and the times we still had ahead of us. We were old, and Jessica was there. She was a mother of two beautiful children — we were grandparents."

I smiled and looked over at Alex. I wasn't sure if he believed the story I was telling him. I knew he had a hard time believing in things that couldn't be proven; he had always been that way.

I remembered something else that could prove I wasn't dreaming, "Alex, I saw my grandfather, and he spoke to me." I reached for Alex's hand, smiling. "It was when you played 'Bad, Bad Leroy Brown.' It was amazing to see him. He was happy. And the candle my mom lit, the one the smelled like the beach — when I smelled it I was overcome by emotion and memories of my aunt Sally, and she came to me."

I looked up at Alex. He looked pale, like he was about to faint. "Alex, are you okay?"

"Jenny, you heard the music? You really heard it? You could smell the candle?" He got up from the chair and started to pace, combing one of his hands through his wavy hair. He looked confused, like he was trying to put all this together. He turned back to me. "You talked to your grandfather and your aunt? It must have been a dream. How could that have happened?" He walked over to the roses he brought the other day. "Yes, I did play that song for you, and you heard it, and we lit the candle and you smelled it. That caused you to dream about them, but you couldn't have really talked to them." Turning around, he asked, "Could you?"

I stood and went to him. "I believe so, Alex. The images and feelings are so strong they feel real." I needed to make him believe me. I held his hand in mine and told him, "I know something that will prove it to you. When I was in the hospital bed in a coma, I was able to hear people talking. I remember some things, not everything. But this I will never forget. Alex, I heard you tell me you went to the chapel and prayed. You prayed for me and our family. You prayed I would live and we would be a family again. I heard you tell me that. Do you remember?" Something about the expression on Alex's face and the way he stood, frozen, told me he did. He was stunned and quiet. As I stared at him I realized he believed what I told him.

"Jenny, it is true. Oh my God, it really happened. You're not imagining things." He held me in his arms. We were overwhelmed by our discovery.

I was glad to know Alex believed me. I was glad that I could remember events surrounding my accident, because for too long I had lived in a time and space where I felt I was alone. I was able to remember more about the time I spent in the hospital, and I understood I hadn't been alone. Each moment, I was with my guardian angel, and she watched over me and guided me while my family watched over me and prayed for me. It was their prayers that she was answering.

My faith in the power of prayer and of a higher being were strengthened by my accident. Through my accident, my husband was able to learn how powerful praying can be. I wouldn't change a thing about the accident on that Sunday afternoon now, knowing it taught Alex to understand he was not in control and it was okay to turn to prayer when he was lost.

Alex

AFTER ONE MONTH IN THE FACILITY, JENNY HAD REGAINED FULL mobility. She was walking and feeding herself—she could do almost everything on her own. Her stamina was getting better, and the nurses and therapists saw improvements every day.

The kids and I prepared the house for Jenny's homecoming. We would finally have her home, just in time for Thanksgiving, and I knew it would be the best Thanksgiving ever.

"Dad, Dad, I think we need tons of balloons." Nicolas was in charge of the decorations.

"And don't forget flowers, Nicolas. Mommy loves flowers, pink and purple ones—and lots of them." Jessica always knew what made her mother happy.

"Okay, guys, put it all on the list."

"Okay." The kids left to the make the homecoming banner and draw welcome-home pictures.

By Monday afternoon the house was decorated from the front door to the back. It resembled a clown's house because Nicolas and Jessica had wrapped everything they could see in paper streamers. We bought two dozen balloons, mostly pink and purple, but Nicolas wanted a couple of yellow ones. He placed them all around the house, inside and out. He tied some pink and purple ones on the mailbox; he tied yellow and pink ones to the door handle on the front door. The rest were scattered throughout the house. He even managed to tie some in my and Jenny's bedroom. There wasn't one room that wasn't drowning in decorations for Jenny's homecoming. The kids had painted banners that read, Welcome home, Mommy, which Jenny would be able to read when she first walked in the door. When she saw them, she would know how much her children loved and had missed her.

I arrived at the rehab center around lunchtime. "Hi, honey. Are you ready for getaway day?"

"Alex, I'm so glad you are here. Can you bring those things to your truck?" Jenny pointed to her belongings, packed and ready to be loaded in my truck.

"I can see you must be feeling like yourself again. We haven't even left yet and you're already ordering me around." She flashed a devilish smile at me and I crumbled. I would do anything for her.

One by one, all Jenny's therapists came to say good-bye and wish her well. When the doctor came by to sign the discharge papers, I could see how much he cared for Jenny. "We are sure going to miss this one. It has been a pleasure getting to know you. I wish all our patients had your tenacity and drive." He turned to shake my hand and then shook Jenny's. "Good luck, Jenny. It has been a real pleasure." I wondered to myself if Jenny ever got tired of the affection people give to her, I had never met anyone who didn't enjoy her company. I smiled, knowing I was a lucky man.

"Let's get out of here," I said as I pushed Jenny's wheelchair down the hall. "It feels like I'm kidnapping you."

"I know. It feels weird to be leaving. I have become so dependent on the staff. What's it going to be like to take care of myself?" She looked up at me, smiling.

"You won't have to know for a while, because I'll be taking care of you now." I placed a kiss on top of Jenny's head.

As we approached the front door, I heard someone calling Jenny's name. When I turned around, I saw a patient walking slowly toward us.

"Jenny, I had to say good-bye and thank you for all your help. I don't think I could have had the strength to push through my pain without your support."

"Oh, Tracey, I'll miss you. You have all the strength you need. You just need to believe in yourself. Soon it will be your day to go home. Take care of yourself, and don't give up." As they shared a hug, I noticed a tear fall from Tracey's eye, but Jenny didn't see it.

The drive home was reminiscent of when I drove Nicolas and Jessica home from the hospital. All I wanted was to pull into the driveway and know we all got home safe. The feeling was even stronger that day with Jenny, and I was relieved when we pulled into our driveway.

Jenny was surprised to see all the balloons and cars. "What is all this?"

"Oh, it's been a while since you've been outside. Fall came, and all the leaves have fallen off the trees." I said, teasing. I turned to Jenny with a smile.

"No! I mean what is with all the cars in the driveway and all the balloons? You guys didn't have to do this."

"Well, this is nothing. Prepare yourself for what is inside."

She looked over at me. "Really? The kids, right?"

"They really missed you. They've been planning for this day for a week."

"That's sweet. I can't wait to see it."

We pulled into the garage, and I let out a deep sigh. "We got you home." I leaned over and kissed Jenny. It was good to have her here. With our parents' help, I knew the house was ready for Jenny's arrival.

Jenny walked in the front door, and everyone yelled, "Welcome home!"

"Oh, my—look at this place! You didn't forget to decorate one thing, did you?" Jenny said, hugging Nicolas and Jessica. "Thank you, guys. It looks beautiful in here. You must have worked really hard on this."

"Welcome home, Mommy."

I helped Jenny walk to the couch. Once she was sitting down, she got hugs from our parents. The kids curled up on one side, leaving a spot for Ann to sit next to her daughter.

"It's good to see you home, honey." Ann sat next to Jenny and held her hand.

"Thanks, Mom. It will take me awhile to get used to being here, but I already notice how much quieter it is compared to the hustle in the rehab center."

"Oh, give it time. These two will be raising the roof soon enough."

Nicolas and Jessica wore mischievous smiles as they looked at their mom.

Jenny

WE PREPARED FOR THANKSGIVING ALL WEEK. WE ALL DECIDED WE would host both of our families at our house because it would be easier for me to be at home. Having everyone gathered together would be a wonderful way to celebrate the holiday. We had a lot to be thankful for this year.

Alex tackled cooking the turkey. My parents and Paul, with his family, arrived first, bringing all the sides: mashed potatoes and gravy, green beans, butternut squash, stuffing, and carrots. Alex's parents and sister dropped off the hors d'oeuvres and desserts before taking all the cousins to run in the holiday road race.

"Hello. We're here." My family came through the door.

"Come in, Mom. We're in the kitchen." I sat at the island, and Alex stood on the other side.

"Oh, Jenny, don't you look beautiful! Seeing you sit in your kitchen is great. I wonder how long it will take me to get used to seeing that."

"Thanks, Mom." I hugged her. "I know what you mean. It feels so different to be home, not in the hospital or rehabilitation center. I'm definitely more comfortable here."

"Happy Thanksgiving, Alex. It's good to see you again."

"Happy Thanksgiving to you, Ann. Is there more food in the car? I can go get it. Sit with Jenny."

"Mom, sit here." I cleared a space for her. "How are you?"

"Knowing you're home makes me happy. It took so long, Jenny. I prayed for you, and even Alex prayed. He spent more time in the chapel then any of us."

"Mom, this all really changed him, didn't it?"

"Yes, it did. Just before you were about to be discharged from the hospital, Alex brought your dad and me to the chapel. He was excited to show us where he went when he wanted to disappear for a while. Jenny, he has a peace about him I've never seen before. He's a bit more relaxed."

My mom and I folded the dinner napkins as we talked.

"I thought he seemed different. I haven't been able to put my finger on it. I guess I put him through a lot, didn't I?" Hearing the words out loud made my chest feel full, heavy. I had thought them many times over the past month, but I'd never said anything to anyone about my feelings. I never wanted to hurt the man who had helped make all my dreams come true. I thought about what it must have been like for Alex to watch while I lay motionless in the hospital for more than two weeks. Knowing how close he came to losing the person closest to him must have been like watching himself die. I shook my head. It was too heavy a thought for today. *It's Thanksgiving, and I should be celebrating that I'm home and healthy.*

Looking around my kitchen, I remembered the sleepless nights and endless hours I'd spent here before my accident. The dark memories of those nights had carried over to the daylight hours, casting a cloud of negative energy that I would try to dismiss as I moved through my days.

As our families gather together today to celebrate the holiday, my view is beginning to change; my kitchen now represents a place of love and peace.

"Mom, can you remember the day I told you about my fears and my sleeplessness, over the idea of losing Alex? You were the only person I talked to about that. I look back now after the accident and understand that the fears I had were nothing more than my thoughts running wild and my body beginning to change."

"Jenny, it's normal to have concerns about losing the people we love most. That's what makes the time we share together so important."

My eyes danced around the room, stopping every so often to gaze on an object or a picture on the refrigerator. I looked at the window sill above the kitchen sink. I got lost in looking at a figurine my grandmother had bought for Alex and me when we moved into our apartment. I'd placed the figurine of a girl holding a bouquet of flowers above the sink in the apartment, and when I moved into our new home, I made a spot for her on the sill above the sink. Sometimes, when I did the dishes and felt lost, I would talk to the girl and remember my grandmother's spirit; it would fill me with love. The little girl clutching the bouquet of flowers in her arms reminded me to hold tight to those things we cherish, and to have faith that everything will be all right.

But today as I stare at her, I am reminded of the difficulties Alex and I faced that day in the apartment kitchen when the house wasn't yet ready for us to move into. I smiled. My mother noticed and asked, "Jenny, what is it? What's on your mind?"

"I'm just remembering something special, Mom. That's all." My private thoughts rush back to that day. Alex was so upset about not being able to move into the house. I recalled telling him that he needed to have faith that situations in life happen for reasons we sometimes never know. I had prayed that night in bed that he would find his way to believe and have faith in a power larger than himself.

I watched Alex as he walked back into the kitchen with Paul. They were carrying armloads of food for the feast we would be serving. As Alex placed the food on the counter, he turned and smiled at me. With a sweet expression, he asked, "What are you looking at?"

"My husband! Is there anything wrong with that?"

What I didn't tell him was that I was filled with love when I looked at him. He was the boy I fell in love with when I was sixteen; the boy who almost broke my heart when he went off to college; the man I discovered deeper love with, the one I decided to spend the rest of my life with, the father of my endearing children. He was the perfect partner. When I looked at him I knew I would be okay. My life would be fine because he was in it, by my side. In keeping the faith my grandmother taught me to have, and considering what my husband and I had been through, we both now knew that, in the end, faith is what gets you through.

***

Questions for the reader

1. Do you believe that Jenny and Alex's relationship could have lasted if Jenny didn't transfer to Michigan State?

2. Would you have transferred to the college your significant other attended to keep your relationship alive?

3. Jenny was in her twenties when her aunt died and left a hole in her life. In Jenny's out-of-body experience, her Aunt Sally came to her.

    a. Do you believe in out-of-body experiences?

    b. Who would you like to see again if you had a similar experience?

4. If you were Alex and suddenly your spouse began treating you differently, as Jenny did, how would you feel?

5. What do you think the doves outside the hospital window represent?

6. What is the significance of the yellow balloons Nicolas wanted at his mother's welcome home party?

7. Who was your favorite character? Why?

8. What emotions did the story evoke in you the reader?

9. What are your thoughts about the relationship between the woman in white in the chapel and Jenny's guardian angel?

10. How has this reading affected your own feelings about faith?

11. Have you had a life-changing experience? How did that transform your outlook on life or your behaviors?

12. How do you respond to adversity?

13. When challenges impact relationships, what causes some couples to come closer together and others to take a step back?

Acknowledgements

Writing this book has been a dream of mine from an early age. For various reasons I always talked myself out of it, but then Life stepped in and pushed me to believe in myself. After having surgery, I started on a seemingly endless reading jaunt. I would go to the library in search of a particular book, and when it wasn't on the shelf I would wander down the aisle eyeing all the spines of the endless stacks. One day, my eyes stopped on the beautiful colored spine of Tracey Garvis Graves' book, *On the Island*. The cover was intriguing. Yes, we do judge books by their covers. After reading *On the Island*, and learning that Tracey wrote it early in the morning hours before her day job, I began to think I could do it too. Jenny and Alex were born in my mind and their story unfolded like a flower blooming with spring's first warmth. It has been a deep pleasure for me to discover their story and bring it to life. I challenged myself to write a book, and never stopped pushing forward until it was complete.

In the beginning, Julie my writing instructor encouraged me by telling me that "people need to hear my voice." She gave me the confidence to pursue my dreams with her words of encouragement.

Along the way, I connected with Sandra McGee, who, like me, dreamed of the day she would apply her writing talents in the form of a book. Sandra helped me through the cobwebs of story-lines and plot troubles. I will be forever grateful for the support she gave me and the replies to the endless emails I sent looking for answers. We have built each other up, and as we say "we are doing this."

Once my job of writing and initial editing was complete, I was so fortunate to find my editor, Sue Ducharme of TextWorks-EquiText to help polish the material. She brought a sparkle to the words through her amazing editing talents. Thank you, Sue.

To my amazing beta-readers, Juliet and Liz, thank you for your time, honesty, and questioning to fine-tune my thoughts and expressions. If the saying goes "four eyes are better than two," well then six eyes are superior to four!

Props to my make-up artist, Christine Galatis, for transforming me for my photos. My amazing photographer, Cristen Farrell at Cristenfarrellphotography.com, created beautiful images in her sunny studio.

My cover artist, Gabrielle Prendergast at coveryourdreams.net, had enormous patience to handle the control-freak inside of me. Thank you! She turned a simple photo into a work of art, and she nailed it!

Guido Henkel, at Guidohenkel.com, formatted the manuscript for the e-book and paperback, and did an amazing job.

Last, but not least, thank you to my amazing, supportive family. Abby and Brendan, thank you for your patience and understanding when I had to lock myself in my office to write; you can have your mother back now. I love you, monkeys. Mike, you are the best husband and friend a girl could ask for. You have been by my side for so many years, witnessing all my dreams coming true; your support means the world to me and I love sharing my life with you.

To my ever powerful and amazing God. Through You, all things are possible. Our story has been told. Amen.